Broken
By
Kings

By

Dr. Jeri Fink

Photography by Dr. Jeri Fink and Richard Fink
Cover and book design by Derek Murphy
Illustrations by Dr. Sandra Roth

Broken By Kings
Written By Dr. Jeri Fink
Photographs By Dr. Jeri Fink

Book and cover design By Derek Murphy

Published By Book Web Publishing, LTD
Copyright © 2016 By Dr. Jeri Fink
All Rights reserved

ISBN-13: 978-1-941882-13-9

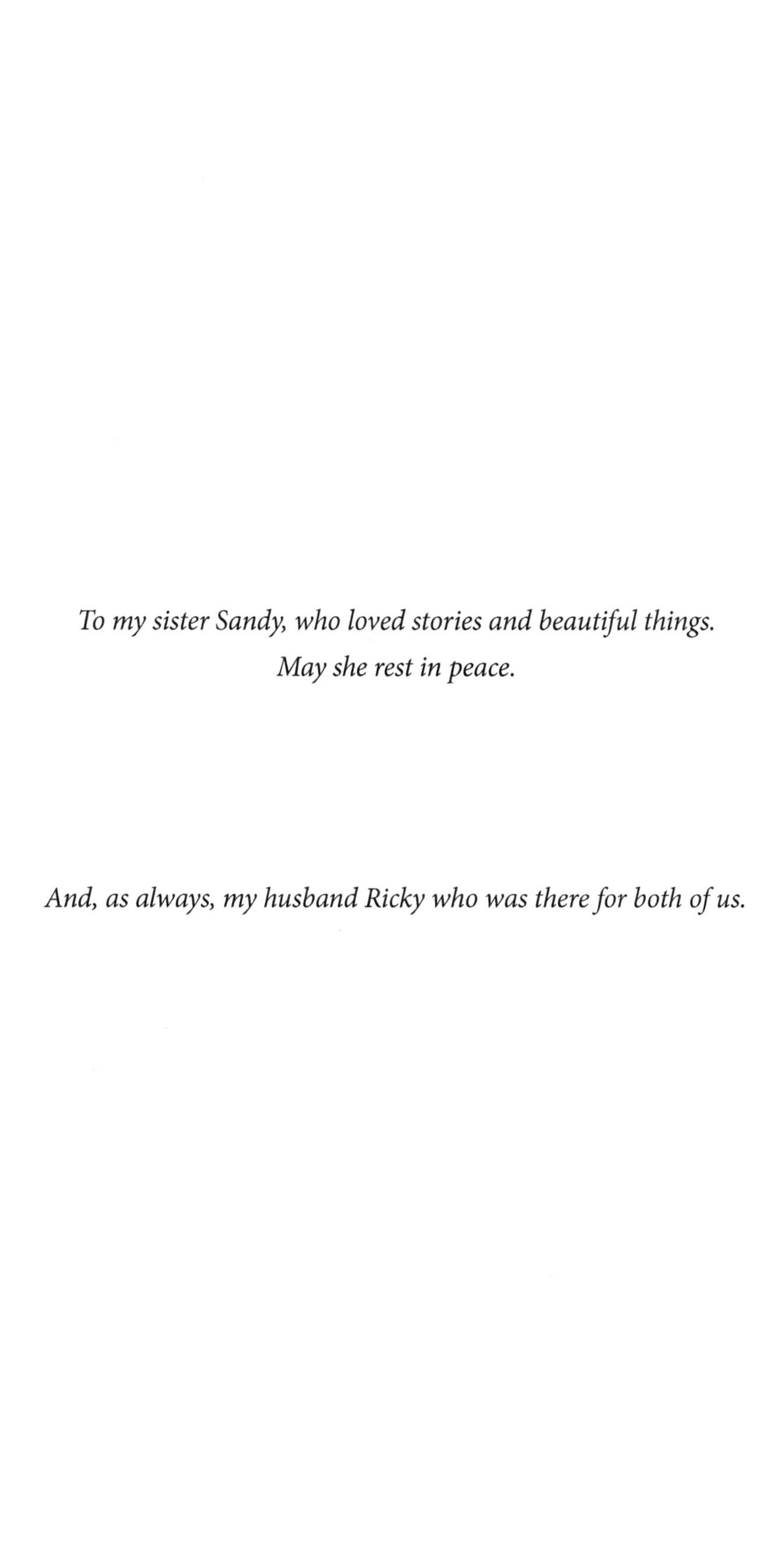

To my sister Sandy, who loved stories and beautiful things.
May she rest in peace.

And, as always, my husband Ricky who was there for both of us.

Check out more *Broken* books written by Dr. Jeri Fink:

Broken By Truth

Broken By Birth

Broken By Evil

Broken By Madness

Broken By Men

Broken: The Prequel

To Purchase books go to:

hauntedfamilytrees.com/books

or

amazon.com

Is there a psychopath in your life? Go to

http://hauntedfamilytrees.com/
haunted-family-trees-landing/

to sign up for your FREE copy of Dr. Fink's ground-breaking guide.

Discover the secrets of haunted family trees – from the infamous to your own . . . Go to

http://hauntedfamilytrees.com/
haunted-family-trees-landing/

to get stories that will amaze you, the truth in facts and photos, and the latest info about family curses and bizarre behavior.

Do you love photo insights? Go to:

http://hauntedfamilytrees.com/
landing-page

to get a free image each week in your email that will enlighten, inspire, and make you feel good.

Broken

By

Kings

1492-1494

Esperanza

1

Our fate was sealed long before I was born.

We lived in hiding, deep within dark tunnels and secret rooms – constantly afraid that prying neighbors, jealous businessmen, angry friends or disloyal servants would see through our deception. It was a necessary double life. Our souls were split from within, forced to move through life with double identities. The fear of discovery was passed from parent to child until we became the prey of snakes hiding in the alleys.

Each family had their own story. For us it began in 1391 with the massacre in Seville. The Jews had enjoyed freedom since King James I conquered Valencia in 1238. He assigned a large quarter or *Judería* to them. Jews, Muslims, and Christians lived in peace. A century later, the Archdeacon of Ecija, Don Fernando Martinez started preaching against the Jews. In July, a mob rushed into the Judería and slaughtered Jewish men, women, and children – slitting their throats in homes and synagogues. Four thousand people were murdered.

It was an old story with new names.

The Jews asked for protection from the King but he was only eleven years old.

Martinez' campaign spread and ten thousand Jews were massacred in Barcelona. That was where my ancestors lived. They were given a choice: conversion or death.

They *tried* to refuse conversion. They were brought to the baptismal font along with others from the Jewish Quarter. They had six children and vowed to honor the Laws of Moses. The priest demanded conversion. They resisted.

Perhaps if only their lives were threatened they wouldn't have given in. I liked to believe that. It was something else when their children were taken.

The soldiers killed their oldest son first.

They watched his small head hacked from his body and roll across the plaza leaving a trail of fresh blood.

I heard their wails in *my soul* – felt their agony as their second son was wrenched from their arms. They didn't believe that *anyone* could slaughter a second innocent child.

They were wrong.

My ancestors accepted baptism. They and their remaining four children became New Christians – *Cristianos Nuevos* – over the blood and decapitated heads of their two eldest sons. They were called *anusim* – forced Christian converts.

Their third son would have been the next to die. My father was directly descended from him. If he had been killed me, my father, and one hundred years of our bloodline would never have existed.

Now it was my turn. It was 1492 and the Inquisition soldiers had come for us.

We were *Conversos* – secret Jews. We prayed in church and professed our loyalty to The Lord and Savior Jesus Christ. When no one was looking, deep beneath the streets of our home, my family secretly followed our legacy – the Laws of Moses – a crime punishable by death in Catholic Spain. Publically, we would have been cursed as *Marranos,* the word for swine.

The two beheaded little boys lived on through us.

No one knew. At least we *believed* that no one knew until the Inquisition soldiers slammed their weapons against our door. Mama and Papa had been ready for their entire lives.

Our lives were complicated. We met with other Conversos – Secret Jews – to follow our Jewish faith beneath the ancient streets of our town. Our prayer books and treasures were hidden in a community room connected by dark, damp tunnels. We passed through the tunnels regularly, guided by flickering lamps that tossed strange, dreamlike shadows against the walls. Our underground world was a covert site that thrived beneath the busy homes and stores of our neighbors. Even my closest friends, like Isabel, who sat devoutly next to me in the large, cavernous church where I prayed to another God, had no idea. They thought we were all Cristianos, worshipping Jesus Christ beneath the gold and crystal of the church, under the watchful eyes of the priests and each other. We prayed on our knees, celebrated holidays, disdained the Jewish Sabbath, wore crosses around our necks, and sent one family member in each generation to a convent or monastery to prove our faith.

It was a crazy disguise.

We were never who we appeared to be – concealing deadly secrets in our souls.

2

The Inquisitors were at our door. We had been betrayed.

I had to move. *Now.* I couldn't take a step.

Mama stared at me, holding her breath. Seconds were transformed into a lifetime.

"The lives that we knew are over," she said too calmly.

"They can't be."

"It's not our choice. We can't stop what was meant to be. The only thing we can do is save you."

We had a good life.

"What happened?"

I knew that when my sister and I escaped into the dark, secret tunnel beneath our home, we faced a deadly truth: someone had turned us in to the Holy Office of the Inquisition. We would never know *who*. Perhaps it didn't matter.

In 15th century Spain infidels and heretics were identified by their refusal to comply with every miniscule law of Christianity. All Jews were the enemy of the soul, the companions of Satan, and the killers of Christ. Christians who secretly practiced Judaism were the worst – *Judaízers* who betrayed the faith. If discovered or turned in, Conversos faced torture and death by fire through The Holy Inquisition. The hated priest Tomás Torquemada, led the charge through Queen Isabella and King Ferdinand. We lived each day in fear that someone might betray us. The burden of carrying two souls, Christian and Jewish, terrified of being reported, exposed by our neighbors, friends or enemies, was crushing.

Suddenly I was a betrayer of the faith – a Judaízer controlled by Satan. My fate was sealed.

The procedure was simple. The monks would take me and my family to the dungeons and torture us until we confessed. I heard about the tortures – words whispered behind trembling hands.

There was the strappado and the rack. Another favorite, the pear, was inserted into a woman's privates; other "tools" like the breast ripper and head crusher were legendary. Judaizers were tortured until confession, conviction, and burned live at the stake in a public celebration called *Auto de Fey* – act of faith.

I was terrified.

They said it was in service of Christ. It seemed more like in service of jealous neighbors, crafty businessmen, and zealous priests. But what did I know? I was only a child. And like all our neighbors I attended Auto de Feys since I was very little, cheering to *prove* our faith. Not attending an Auto de Fey was a giveaway.

Mama and Papa, unlike many of their ancestors, were not going to let their children die.

"We'll be your decoy," Papa said sharply as he shoved the heavy table across the floor, rolled up the thick carpet beneath, and exposed the trap door. "Live and continue the seed of our family."

He raised the trapdoor and I saw steps disappearing into darkness.

I couldn't leave and I couldn't stay.

Papa handed Hanna a worn leather pouch filled with coins. "Take this," he ordered, his voice choked with tears. Papa had been prepared.

"Esperanza," my mother demanded, "go."

Go?

"I can't."

"Here," she put something around my neck. Mama had been prepared too. "My spirit is in this. I'll protect you from wherever I am. When it's your time, give it to someone you love very much.

Someone who needs its protection. We will always keep it among us to remember – remember what happened here today."

"No."

"You have the red hair and hazel eyes. It *has* to be yours."

I lost my voice. Mama forced me to the edge of the steps.

"The tunnel," Hanna cried. "We have to get to the tunnel."

Mama shoved me onto the steps. "No," I cried but it was too late. I was in the gloom, Hanna pulling me down into the dark. Papa snapped the trap door over our heads and we were engulfed in black. Hanna raised the lamp in her shaky hands.

I screamed.

Hanna's free hand covered my mouth. "Listen," she whispered. "Stay quiet."

I squirmed away and pushed her, refusing to be tamed.

"Stop," Hanna said in a voice I never heard before. "Listen and keep quiet."

I heard the door to our home break and imagined splinters of wood flying in all directions. Gruff male voices filled our home. There were footsteps above our heads, men laughing, things breaking, the sound of Papa thrown to the floor, howling in pain as they beat him. Mama's screams, the sound of cloth ripping . . . what were they doing to Mama?

Mama was a beautiful woman with red hair and hazel eyes like me.

"No," I cried but it was just an agonizing whimper.

Hanna put her arms around me in the darkness. I buried my head in her breasts. "I never said 'I love you.' I never said 'goodbye.'"

"You didn't have to. They knew."

My face was wet with tears. I was a coward – I ran instead of protecting my parents. I slapped my forehead and Hanna caught my hand.

"You didn't do anything wrong. Mama and Papa knew – they were ready. They gave their lives for us."

It sounded oddly like the words said in church – *Jesus Christ gave his life for you.*

I shrugged off the thought as Hanna took my hand and led me deeper into the gloom. "We have to go, that's what Mama and Papa wanted."

I sobbed although I knew she couldn't hear.

3

Hanna and I had been in the tunnel many times with Mama and Papa. Every holiday, every celebration of our Jewish *selves* began there. Now we were alone. Sisters commanded to survive.

We followed the walls, trying not to think of the vermin that lived underground. The dark was like a black robe thrown over our heads. The only light came from Hanna's tiny lamp. The tunnel went deeper until we were too far underground to hear much except our footsteps. The air was cold and damp. I tasted the musty flavor of age and ancient secrets. We kept on going towards the fork in the tunnel.

Papa's voice rang in my head like a children's rhyme, his singsong words repeated so I wouldn't forget. "Right without doubt, left to get out."

Papa explained the rhyme. "If you go right at the fork you'll find our hidden community room with sacred books, garments, and precious Jewish treasures. Left if you need to escape. The left tunnel ends at a door that opens to the outside beyond the city walls."

Right without doubt, left to get out.

I used to think he was silly. It was a game – a scary story that could never come true. We would never need to get out. My family was the perfect *Conversos,* working every Saturday on the Jewish Sabbath and attending church every Sunday on the Christian Sabbath. We were never far from a crucifix or rosary. Papa had a cousin who was a priest and papers that attested to our family's one hundred years as New Christians – Jews who had embraced the faith of Jesus Christ. We would live forever in Spain; no one would know our secret.

I caught my breath.

That was over. We were on the run – fleeing the Inquisition, torture, burned live at the stake . . .

I shivered.

"We'll join the expelled Jews," Hanna intruded. "We won't be Conversos any more."

I had to embrace her words. How?

"Say these secret words," Mama had instructed me when I was little. "Say them when you're scared. The God of Moses will help you."

They emerged as a whisper in the gloom.

Shema Yisrael Adonai Elohaenu Adonai Echad
Hear O Israel The Lord is God, The Lord is One.

The words gave me courage although I didn't know exactly *why*.

We continued as I listened to the imaginary voices of people who went before us, whooshing robes guarding their perch in the past. The dead were as alive as the living. An icy chill ran down my back.

"How are we going to survive?"

"Ssssssh. Papa gave me coins. We'll find a way."

"I'm tired."

"Oh, Esperanza." Hanna turned and hugged me. "I'm tired too but we have to do this. It was Mama and Papa's last request."

"Last?"

She was silent. I closed my eyes although it made little difference in the dark. I took a deep breath and tried to slow my racing heart.

Right without doubt, left to get out.

The minutes stretched endlessly. My feet hurt and I was tired and cold. I wanted to lay on the damp dirt floor and go to sleep. Hanna wouldn't allow it.

"We have to keep going. Can't stop."

She was right. Suddenly we faced a damp stone wall in front of us. We were at the fork. *Right without doubt, left to get out.* Right to our past, left to our future.

"Left," Hanna's voice was soft and sad. "*Adios.*"

Hanna held my hand as we took the left fork that led out of the only home we had ever known.

4

The left fork was rough, the tunnel narrow with rocks and pebbles scattered across the path. Few people had ever used it. We slowed our pace, careful not to twist an ankle. The lamp in Hanna's hands flickered as if blown by a supernatural wind. It felt like the walls were closing in as if they would eventually meet and crush us to death.

"It's okay," Hanna tried to say confidently. It didn't work. Her voice was high-pitched and quivering. "Papa said it would be okay."

I believed Hanna and I believed Papa but I was terrified. I don't know how long we spent in the left-side tunnel but it felt like most of the night. We were slow, we were wary, and we were two frightened children.

Suddenly my foot struck a stone wedge. Hanna and I froze.

"We're here. At the steps."

"I don't want to go ahead."

"Where do you want to go?"

"Back. To Mama and Papa."

"We can't go back ever again. That part of our lives is over. We can remember it in our hearts – remember Mama and Papa – but we'll never see them again, live in our house, and have Friday night dinners . . ."

Hanna's eyes glistened in the light from the lamp. She was crying. I hugged her tightly. "You're so brave. I wish I was brave like you. You got us here and you'll get us to wherever we need to go. You and I are sisters and we'll take care of each other. I promise. We'll never leave each other. Nothing can tear us apart."

Hanna nodded but it was clear she didn't believe me. "The steps," she sighed. "Let's do the steps."

I squeezed her hand and we made our way up the ancient rock steps. My heart pounded crazily. What if the Inquisitors were waiting for us at the top? Where would we run?

We reached the door. Hanna and I were silent as we struggled to push it open. Cobwebs stuck to us like silky strings, coating my red hair with a lacey net. Finally the door relented and fresh air washed across our faces. We stepped outside into a peaceful night with a full moon. There was an eerie glow over the countryside. A dirt trail led away from the door to the edge of the forest. The trail hadn't been used for a long time and was filled with weeds and rocks.

"Papa told me that the trail goes through the forest, up a hill, and ends on the main road out of town. They'll be a lot of Jews on the road obeying the *Edict of Expulsion*. They didn't have much time to pick up and leave their homes. The King's soldiers have vowed to kill those who haven't been baptized."

"Where are they going?"

"Portugal or the ships."

"What does that mean?"

"Oh Esperanza, don't you listen? Papa told us that the exiled Jews could cross the border into Portugal and pay an entrance fee. Jews could also take a ship that sailed for places across the big water but that was more dangerous."

"What places?"

"I'm not sure. Some go to the Ottoman Empire. Others to Morocco and Africa."

"Where's Africa?"

"I don't know – it's very far away from us. People with black skin live there."

"Like the Moors?"

"Yes, like the Moors. Now let's stop asking questions and rest when we have the chance."

We found a rock hidden in the brush. It was big enough for us to lie on without being seen. Hanna closed her eyes.

I couldn't sleep. Instead, I touched the charm that Mama gave me. It was her hamsa – a silver hand crafted in delicate filigree with three uplifted fingers and two thumbs. An "eye" or blue stone in the middle stared unblinkingly out at the world. Mama always wore it around her neck. I heard her voice in my head as if she was next to me.

"Hamsa is ancient. The word comes from the Aramaic. It means five – five fingers or a hand. It keeps away the angel of death. Some say it's the hand of Miriam – the sister of Moses. Others believe it's the protective hand of God. It draws positive energy – life and happiness – and repels the evil eye. I always wore it around my neck, like you'll wear it someday. Then you'll pass it on to protect some one you love very much. Perhaps your own daughter."

I carefully slipped the hamsa beneath my clothes so no one could see. I stared at the moon trying to figure out what was happening to us. And why?

There were no answers.

5

We slept. A few hours later we pushed forward. The sky was getting lighter and we didn't want to linger in an exposed area. The forest loomed before us. Trusting Papa's instructions that the trail would lead us far away from home and the Inquisitors, we sang *Right without doubt, left to get out* and headed for the trees. The fresh air gave us hope. Maybe we could pull this off?

"Where are we going?" I asked Hanna.

"The Road to Portugal. King Ferdinand kicked out all the Jews. He signed the *Alhambra Decree* or *Edict of Expulsion* in Granada four months ago. It said that all Jews had to convert or leave. They could only bring a few things with them, leaving homes, businesses, animals, and one thousand years of life in Spain."

I looked at her quizzically.

"Most left, of course. It didn't apply to Conversos like us. No one knew we were Jewish."

"Until someone reported us to the Holy Office of The Inquisition."

"Yes. So now we're no longer Conversos – just Jews. And we have to leave along with the others."

It felt like I was putting on new clothes.

"Think of it this way, Esperanza. We're two Jewish girls among hundreds of thousands of people. No one will notice us."

We reached the trees. We heard the sounds of approaching dawn – birds, night animals seeking cover, insects buzzing, leaves and branches crackling with invisible creatures. I felt safer. The dirt was rough and uneven, forcing us to walk carefully, eyes on the ground. The air was cold and we shivered in our thin summer clothes. I was scared but refused to admit it. Neither of us spoke.

The sun was high in the sky and lighting up the forest, when we finally reached the last hill. We clamored up and there it was – the Road to Portugal. It seemed endless each way we looked.

"We don't know enough." I frowned.

"They didn't have time to teach us. We'll have to learn on our own."

I thought of Mama and Papa who sacrificed their lives so we could escape The Inquisitors. Where were they now?

Hanna found a few boulders on the edge of the road.

"Hide behind them," she pointed. "No one will see us. We'll spend the night here."

"Why do we have to be scared of the Jews? We're one of them."

"You never know. We have to be careful of anyone and anything."

Hungry and tired, we curled up behind the boulders. Sleep came grudgingly, making me wonder if I would ever feel safe again. Visions of Mama and Papa filled my head. They were already in the dungeons. Perhaps the priests had started the tortures. Perhaps Mama was so numb from the assault that she didn't feel anything? I prayed that God would take care of them.

After a few hours we heard sounds from the road. I peered between the rocks and discovered the most remarkable sight I had ever seen.

Hundreds, maybe thousands of people passed before us.

Rich people, dressed in fine clothes made from costly fabrics led the way on large, spirited horses. They were followed by a sea of old, creaky carts with wooden wheels, piled high with household possessions, bundles of clothing and food – all pulled by straining donkeys. Men cajoled the donkeys to move forward. Some tried to whip the animals with switches but it was clear that the people had no stomach for hurting animals. Instead, they snapped the switches over the animal's heads, hoping to startle them into motion. Small children and old people were wedged between piles of stuff in the carts, swaying with the motion, steadying their possessions when they crossed ruts in the dirt road. Others walked – children, young men, mothers carrying babies, men and women hunched over with huge packs on their backs, and the tired and disabled who had to struggle to keep up. Some men walked and read prayers. They spoke Ladino and said their prayers in Hebrew. Older children played games, leaping like cats around the adults, finding small rocks and dried branches to use as toys.

Suddenly a group of monks appeared. They looked wild-eyed in their brown hooded robes, weaving between the people on the road. In a strange, haunting chorus they shouted "repent, repent, it's your last chance to be saved by Jesus Christ." Waving thick, heavy crucifixes, they leaped into the throng of Jews.

"You're following the path to Satan," one shouted, his voice hoarse with the effort. "Denounce the devil and join the love of God."

The Jews got angry. They had left everything behind them to honor the Laws of Moses. The sweaty monks accused them of devil worship. It was intolerable.

A young Jewish man with wavy blond hair turned to the exiles. "Sing," he cried, "sing unto the Lord for His everlasting grace! Show them that we're the proud and strong Children of Israel!"

A few people began to sing a sweet, haunting melody. Others caught on. In a few minutes *everyone* joined – their voices rose in a Ladino song. Young men and women entered the fray, dancing, playing timbrels or small drums, waving tambourines or clapping their hands. Caught in the energy, children scampered to the rhythms. Even the animals pulled harder. Everyone responded to the wildly infective music.

Give to the Lord
Honor and glory,
Give to the Lord
The glory of the divine name.

The Lord will give strength to his people
The Lord will bless his people
With peace.

"Refuse," the rabbis called above the music, "sing and uplift your souls."

The monks were desperate as their voices were drowned out by the music, songs, and cavorting Jews.

"They're exiles," Hanna whispered, "and they still sing?"

The monks gave up. They lowered their crosses and retreated down the road, searching for another throng of exiled Jews. The Jews cheered, held their heads high, and continued down the Road to Portugal.

We watched in awe.

"The Jews," Hanna mumbled, "leave Spain proudly with dignity."

Could I ever be that brave?

I knew that once, a long time ago, Jews, Christians and Moslems all lived together. King Ferdinand and Queen Isabella changed that. Papa once told me that Jews were called *the chosen people* not because they were given money, fine clothes, and great abilities. Rather, Jews were chosen to take on the burdens of humankind, to bear the very best, the very worst, and everything in-between – to face life with the faith and determination of thousands of years of thought, law, and faith in the Jewish soul. Being "chosen" was a responsibility not a luxury.

I thought about Papa's words as I watched the Jews. Now it was our turn to be one with them, destined to leave Spain. Five generations of secrets ended on a dusty road that led away from home and the Inquisitors.

Hanna and I held hands as we watched the flow of Jews headed for Portugal.

Hanna

1

The next morning we started down the road that led to the city of Lisboa in Portugal.

Hanna and I followed groups of Jews. We kept a slow, steady pace and made sure we didn't fall behind. No one noticed – we were two small, strange faces lost in an exodus.

"Is this like the exodus of Jews from Egypt?" I asked Hanna.

She shrugged. "I think so. Maybe the tunnel was like Moses crossing the Red Sea?"

We laughed.

We spotted a man on the roadside selling baskets of stale bread and cheese. Hanna dug out a few coins from the leather pouch. I patted my hamsa as she bargained for the food. Where did she learn to do that? Mama never taught me. Hanna secured the basket.

We sat by the side of the road beneath an old, twisted tree.

"Eat."

"I'm not hungry."

"You have to eat or you'll lose your strength. You won't be able to make it to Portugal."

"My feet hurt."

Hanna laughed. "So do mine."

We finished our meal and joined the throngs back on the road. Hours later we began to see the dead on the edge of the road.

"They couldn't make it," Hanna whispered. "They were too weak or too old or too sick. They couldn't survive the journey to Portugal."

I stared at the groups surrounding the dead. Shallow graves were ringed by men saying prayers, women and children crying, and friends and once-neighbors watching as their loved one was buried. The wood carts paused and the donkeys were content to wait in the blistering sun.

The truth was ugly. No one cared about a dead Jew.

We paused behind a large group of mourners. Ten men surrounded the gravesite.

"It's called a *minyan*," Hanna explained. "Death is a natural process, part of God's plan. Jews need a minyan – ten men over the age of thirteen – to say the Mourner's *Kaddish*, or prayer for the dead. First, they put a small tear in the family's clothing on the right side of their chests. It represents mourning."

I noticed the torn clothing on the people that surrounded the gravesite.

"One of the greatest *mitzvahs* or good deeds a Jew can do is to say the Mourner's Kaddish. It's a good deed because the dead can't repay you for your kindness – there's no expectation of earthly reward. It's also a good deed because you're elevating a soul – helping one move to a higher realm."

How did Hanna know? Did she listen to Mama and Papa when I was out playing with Isabel and Palo?

The minyans said their words in haunting prayers that resounded within me.

Yit'gadal v'yit'kadash sh'mei raba
May His great Name grow exalted and sanctified

b'al'ma di v'ra khir'utei
in the world that He created as He willed.

v'yam'likh mal'khutei b'chayeikhon uv'yomeikhon
May He give reign to His kingship in your lifetimes and in your days,

uv'chayei d'khol beit yis'ra'eil
and in the lifetimes of the entire Family of Israel,

ba'agala uviz'man kariv v'im'ru:
swiftly and soon. Now say:

Amein. Y'hei sh'mei raba m'varakh l'alam ul'al'mei al'maya
Amen. May His great Name be blessed forever and ever.

I wondered how people could thank God when He put them on this road and killed their loved ones. I knew the question was blasphemous for either Jew or Christian but I couldn't stop the question.

We moved on. There were more graves and torn clothing. Many Jews died on the road to Lisboa.

The sky darkened and we found a place to sleep alongside the road. Most did the same. Hanna and I whispered to each other for hours, talking about Mama and Papa and the life behind us. I closed my eyes and for a moment it felt like we were home and Mama would yell at us for not going to sleep.

It was only a moment.

2

We woke early the next morning and finished the bread and cheese.

"We'll get more," Hanna said. "There are many Spanish peasants looking to sell food. They make a lot of money from the Jews."

We started down the road, following a new group of people. Something was different – the people were quiet and tense.

"What's happening?"

"We're almost at the border. People are afraid."

"Why?'

"We'll find out."

A few hours later we reached a turn in the road. I couldn't see far ahead until it widened and there was a sight more incredible than the throngs of people on the road.

We were at the border.

The Portuguese soldiers were ready. King Joao II of Portugal welcomed the Jews into his land with certain caveats. Each family was charged one hundred *cruzados*. Only six hundred families were allowed to enter. Each adult was charged eight *cruzados* but could only remain in the country for eight months.

No one kept count. The Jews had to get out of Spain and it was a great opportunity for the soldiers. They stole money, gold, and all the valuable goods that Jews brought with them. Since Portugal was easier to reach from Spain, it was said that up to one hundred and fifty thousand exiled Jews flooded the small country.

I was stunned by what lay before my eyes.

Hundreds . . . thousands of people waited beneath a searing sun. They had no where else to go. The line was long and slow.

The donkeys, hitched to overloaded wooden carts, brayed loudly, objecting to their burdens. Angry adults yelled at one another and occasionally swatted at the donkeys. Children were everywhere, mothers unhappily trying to quiet them. Women wearing black robes of mourning moved like shadows throughout the chaos. Many loved ones had died. Some carts carried hens in shaky wooden coops – food for the travelers. Hungry dogs protected family possessions by pacing back and forth, patrolling the carts, growling, barring their teeth, and barking at anyone who came too close. Scores of exhausted refugees were stretched out on the ground or walked nervously in a blind, rhythmic motion. The sounds merged into an ear-splitting symphony – angry, grief-stricken adults, babies and young children wailing, parents yelling at their families and rabbis desperately trying to soothe the crowd with prayers. Nuns and monks worked the masses, holding up crucifixes, begging for Jesus, promoting salvation through last-minute conversion.

Hanna and I joined the line.

It took the rest of the day to reach the front. The border soldiers were tired and annoyed; they looked at us like we were animal carcasses to be tossed away. They went through the remains of our basket of food and stared suspiciously when we told them we had no possessions.

I trembled inside, praying they didn't see my fear.

The soldiers sneered at two girls traveling alone without men to protect them. They searched our bodies, rifling through our hair, peeking into our mouths, ears, and noses. They thrust their hands into our pockets and tossed away the few bits of remaining bread in our basket.

One soldier wrenched up my skirt to search for gold hidden in my undergarments. He laughed and fondled my privates. I saw they were doing the same to Hanna. Tears filled my eyes but she stared straight ahead as if nothing was happening.

I wanted to be like Hanna.

I endured everything because there was no choice. If I screamed they would be worse, taking pleasure from my distress. If I cried their hands would linger. I closed my eyes and tried to imitate Hanna – pretending not to feel their greedy fingers or the sickening humping on my buttocks like dogs in heat.

Suddenly the soldier found my hamsa. He examined it with his filthy hands, trying to figure out if it had any value.

"*Magica*," I whispered. "Jewish spirits. If you take it from me it will bring you very bad luck. Perhaps even death."

He dropped it quickly and pushed me away. Hanna handed them the entry money. We were done.

Hanna and I clutched hands as we crossed the border. We were in Portugal.

"I saved some coins for us." Hanna whispered.

"How?"

"I put them . . . places they couldn't reach." She patted her belly. "Inside me."

We laughed. Further down the road we found a hollow and settled in beneath the rapidly growing dark. We had no food or water, but for the moment we were safe. Both of us fell into a restless sleep wondering how long it would take for Hanna to pass the coins from her body.

3

It didn't take long. The next day we returned to the road, walking with the crowds until *Castelo de Sao Jorge* loomed above us and Lisboa. It stood high and powerful, as if protecting everyone below. The city grew like wildflowers on the surrounding hills. My heart soared – perhaps this was the end of our escape and the beginning of a new life?

I was a child. I didn't understand how people can be broken by kings.

"We're free," I sang to Hanna.

"Torquemada hates the Jews," she replied, talking about the infamous Inquisitor and author of the expulsion, "and he himself is part Jewish. Why should King Joao be any different?"

Was there ever such a thing as being free? If we could be tossed out of Spain after a thousand years why did I ever think we could trust Portugal?

Hanna tried to bring me back to reality but I still believed *Castelo de Sao Jorge* was magical – our return to peace and safety. With hearts pounding, we followed the masses of exiles trudging up the steep road that led to the castle. A gentle breeze from the harbor encouraged us, helping to ignore the crush of bodies all moving in the same direction. In the distance Lisboa sparkled in the sun, spreading like tree roots from the feet of the castle to the harbor on the Tagus River.

The distance was deceiving.

We arrived and began the climb to the end of the road – the square in front of Castelo de Sao Jorge. There was nothing magical about the web of narrow, twisted streets shadowed by rickety balconies and overhangs. Laundry hung everywhere – clean items suspended in teeming alleys. Many of the heavy wooden doors that opened to the streets were shielded by thick iron gates. The higher we climbed toward the castle, the more we were engulfed in a sea of people. There was more people squeezed into the city than on the road – more people than I had ever seen in my life.

We made our way into the main plaza. Hanna and I froze. It was a sight I will never forget. People were everywhere. Some were curled up on the street, dressed in dirty rags, faces coated with dust. Children cried, ran, played, and stole bits of food. Families claimed tiny pieces of street, living in tight groups and obsessively guarding piles of frayed possessions and stashes of water and food. Carts filled with household goods and thin, emaciated animals were shoved into any corner or gap that could be claimed. Every part of the plaza was occupied, spilling over into the alleys and narrow crevices between buildings. Newcomers desperately searched for small spots amid the chaos. The stench was overwhelming – trash, excrement, urine, dirty water, food carpeted in flies, and sweaty unwashed bodies pressed together in unrelenting heat.

The noise hurt the most – chanting voices echoed by crying adults, mothers with no milk in their breasts desperately trying to nurse howling babies, old men and women pounding their chests begging for help from God, young men feverishly demanding justice, and children playing timeless games untouched by the bedlam that surrounded them.

This was the legacy of the Spanish crown and church.

The people had nothing. Ferdinand and Isabella stole their homes and dignity; Portugal took what little remained. There was no food or water, no shelter or comfort, no place to be clean in the manner that Jews believed. They had been thrust into a living hell on earth.

"We can't stay here," Hanna whispered.

I tore my eyes away from the plaza. "Why?"

"These people will be sick . . . very soon. If we stay, we'll die with them."

"I don't understand."

"Papa told me about the Black Death. This is what it looks like."

"How do you know that?"

Hanna shrugged. "I don't know but we can't stay here."

"Where can we go?"

"I don't know that but we'll die if we stay here."

"Why don't these people *leave?* Protect themselves?"

"They're waiting."

"For what?"

"The ships that King Joao promised. The sanctuary and shelter he promised to provide. He lied. They're waiting for help that won't come."

My hands trembled. How did she *know?*

"No hope." Hanna added.

"There's always hope."

Hanna ignored me. "Let's leave. Now."

"I don't want to leave. I'm tired and hungry and my feet hurt."

"You'll do what I say."

"No!"

"Then stay. I'm leaving."

Hanna turned and pushed against the crowd, away from Castelo de Sao Jorge. I waited for her to change her mind. Her back was stiff. There was no turning around. I screamed and ran after her.

"Don't leave me alone Hanna."

She smiled and offered her hands. "Let's get out of here. Together."

We fought our way back down the road that brought us to Lisboa. It was choked with exiles, flowing into the Lisboa streets, believing that they had found safety. We pushed against the tide of bodies. There were hundreds of them and only two of us so we moved slowly, determined to get beyond the waves of people.

Some people cursed us for going the wrong way. Others tried to convince us to follow the crowd. Hanna was resolute. No one could change her mind and I was too scared to be alone without her.

It took us twice as long to get back to the road to Lisboa as it took to get to the castle. When we reached the bottom of the hill there were fewer people. The crush of bodies, donkeys, and carts lightened. We found a circle of trees off the side of the road and hid. No one saw us. We huddled together – two girls without food, water or anyplace to go.

Sleep found us long after night had settled.

4

The next morning I awoke to the sound of more voices on the road. I peered through the trees and watched them struggle up the hill. They moved like a herd of goats onto a doomed road to Castelo de Sao Jorge.

There was no room left yesterday. Where would they go today?

"There are so many," Hanna whispered from behind me.

I didn't respond.

"We'll find a way."

"We need water," I said softly. "Food – a place to live."

We stared at each other. There would be no tears.

"Let's go to the countryside? Maybe someone will help."

"Then what?"

"I don't know."

We left the trees and started walking back towards Spain.

"Lisboa is that way," a young, bearded man shouted at us, pointing toward Castelo de Sao Jorge.

"Thank you," Hanna said sweetly.

He stared at us quizzically. Finally he shook his head and continued on to Lisboa.

We walked for hours until a narrow dirt trail off the main road caught Hanna's eye.

"Let's try it."

"Are you sure?"

"No – but what other choice do we have? This *feels* right."

We left the road to Lisboa and followed the trail. It meandered through summer-browned grass, pastures, and rocky fields. The noise from the main road faded. Occasionally we passed bleached white houses with red roofs clustered together like a mama with her babies. There were olive trees, small farms and distant, isolated farmhouses. We used our hands to drink from a tiny creek, quenched the awful thirst, washed our faces, and cleaned the dust from our clothes.

Hanna and I walked deep into the Portuguese countryside. We were quiet as we went down the trail, afraid that someone might see us before we saw them. Although we were openly Jewish in a country that promised to accept us, we had to be very careful.

"We don't want to meet any soldiers in the country," Hanna cautioned.

"Dangerous men."

I pictured Mama in my head. So did Hanna. We were so lost in thought that we didn't notice the trail was turning and we couldn't see anything ahead.

An old man startled us.

He blocked the trail, towering over us. We froze. He eyed us with curiosity. The man was old but fearsome, with deep wrinkles cut into his skin, small brown eyes, and a mane of unkempt gray hair. He was painfully thin with the heavy, sagging muscles of a lifetime of hard labor.

He spoke rapidly in Portuguese. The words sounded angry. We didn't understand him.

"*Judio*," Hanna said softly.

The old peasant wrinkled his nose. "*Necesita ayuda?*" He asked in Spanish. Do you need help?

"*Si*," we said together.

The old man smiled.

Aldonca
&
Goncallo

1

It was the beginning of an unlikely friendship between an elderly Christian couple and two young, desperate sisters.

"*Gratissima*." I said one of the few Portuguese words that I knew.

"Goncallo," he replied, pointing to his chest.

"Esperanza," I smiled. "Hanna. *Hermanas*."

Goncallo grinned. "*Yo te ayudare*" I will help you.

Hanna and I looked at each other. Was the old man safe? Where did he want to take us?

"I have a good feeling about him," Hanna whispered.

"Me too – but feelings don't always lead us in the right direction." She shrugged.

"Let's do it – what's the worst that can happen?"

Hanna gave me a strange look but didn't respond.

Goncallo listened, waiting for a decision. "*Vamonos*." He said finally and waved for us to follow. He led us across a meadow with long, brown grass, through a small grove of olive trees, and into a tiny rocky clearing. A very old whitewashed hovel with a bright red roof stood on the edge. Next to it was a tiny open barn with room for a cow, a few chickens, and a donkey.

An old woman appeared in the doorway. She had age-spotted skin and deep wrinkles that covered her entire face. Her clothes were patched and her face was soft like a grandmother. She looked at us kindly.

Goncallo spoke to her in rapid-fire Portuguese. Her eyes widened.

"*Pobrecito*," she said in heavily accented Spanish. "I'm Aldonca. I once lived in Spain and the Jews were very good to me."

I struggled to smile.

Aldonca nodded thoughtfully. "They do terrible things to you, Ferdinand and Isabella. *Demonios.*" She frowned. "You went to Lisboa? *Sí?*"

"Yes."

"Too many people. We hear bad stories."

"I'm afraid."

Aldonca pursed her lips. "We can't do much," she frowned. "We're poor people, peasants whose daughters have married and moved far away. We have very little, barely enough for ourselves. We sell the olives we collect from the grove, drink the milk from the cow, and eat the eggs from the hens . . ." She paused. "We don't have much, but we will share with you. Our donkey recently died so you can sleep in his empty space in the barn. The straw is clean and the cow won't mind."

Hanna and I looked at each other.

"I think it's okay."

"I agree. Let's try it."

Aldonca nodded. "You're safe with us. Now rest, the road makes one weary."

She led us to the donkey's stall next to the cow. The straw was clean and sweet-smelling.

"I loved the animal," Aldonca explained, tears glazing her eyes. "Perhaps he died because he knew you were coming."

Our eyes met. We were safe for the moment. Maybe God really did work in strange ways? Hanna and I stretched out on the straw and immediately fell asleep.

Later, I opened my eyes and the sun burned my vision A black silhouette rose above me. I opened my mouth to scream when the old woman's voice soothed me.

"Don't be afraid. You're safe with us. You must eat."

She left a basket with bread, cheese, and a few olives. "It's not much," she added apologetically, "but it's all we have."

It was a feast for kings.

2

Aldonca and Goncallo treated as if we were their own children. They gave us food and comfort and taught us to speak Portuguese. We settled into the old donkey's stall and made a home from straw. The old couple had little but they shared everything. We learned how to grab eggs from the feisty hens, milk the cow, duck the fierce rooster who hovered over his harem, and pluck olives from the trees. We began to heal. I wondered if we dared hope for a future. How strange that time can cure like a magical potion. We didn't *forget*, instead we eased into our strange new life trying not to think of what was happening to the Jews in Lisboa, where Mama and Papa were, or what would come next for us.

A peasant who fled Lisboa stopped by and brought us the news from the city.

"Black Death has broken out," he grimaced, drinking the cool water Aldonca gave him. "People are sick and dying everywhere. There is much fear." He glared at me. "They blame it on the Jews."

I couldn't sleep that night. The light from the moon filtered into the stall. I watched shadows dance across the straw and asked questions that sent chills through me.

What would have happened if we stayed in Lisboa?

What would have happened if The Inquisitors had found us at the end of the tunnel?

How did Hanna know?

There were no answers. Only more questions.

Over the next few weeks more travelers stopped for food and water, bringing news of the continuing horrors in Lisboa – people succumbing to Black Death, vermin everywhere, rats as large as dogs, and panic. The Jews were blamed for everything. Portuguese youth wandered the streets, beat up Jewish men and raped their women. The Jews banded together but they had no strength or weapons.

The numbers were staggering. Some said 150,000 Jews fled Spain into Portugal – nearly half of all the exiles. No one really knew and rumors ran rampant, reaching into countryside.

We waited.

I wasn't sure what we waited *for.* Times to improve? Jews to become Portuguese citizens without baptism? Some people demanded that King Joao II provide the ships that he had promised to the Jews – ships that would transport us to Africa and Turkey. The King was furious. He decided to teach the Jews a lesson. He provided a ship and filled it up with Jewish refugees. When the ship reached the high seas – where no one could see or hear their cries – the sailors bound the men and forced them to watch their women raped. After the sailors were finished they dumped the Jews on a deserted African beach. Exhausted, spiritually devastated, the children begged for food as the adults dug their graves. They were near death when a group of Moors appeared and seized them, declaring they were now slaves. The local Jews paid exorbitant prices to buy the survivors out of slavery.

The story was leaked. King Joao was successful and the Jews stopped demanding ships. King Joao didn't want to get rid of his Jews – he just wanted to convert them. He was crazy enough to believe that he could succeed where King Ferdinand and Queen Isabella had failed.

When the Jews refused to comply, the King raised the stakes. He claimed that only 600 families were allowed into Portugal and all the others belonged to him.

"That means he *owns* us?" I asked.

Hanna nodded. "Like the Jewish slaves in Egypt."

Aldonca and Goncallo tried to protect us from the stories but more travelers arrived with horrible tales. The travelers were young and old, some fleeing, some searching for a better life, all believing that survival meant leaving Lisboa.

After eight months of welcoming the Jews, King Joao II lost patience. He proclaimed that *all* Jewish exiles in Portugal had to be baptized or become his slaves. He wanted to *keep* the Jews but only as Christians.

"Don't worry," I comforted Hanna. "The soldiers won't find us here."

A few days later a new story arrived from Lisboa, carried by a traveler headed for Spain. His skin was scarred with pox marks and his greasy dark hair fell loosely over his face. He stared at Hanna's breasts as he spoke.

"I heard," he said, wiping Aldonca's cheese from his beard and licking his lips with a thick, red tongue, "that there's a small uninhabited island off the west coast of Africa, discovered and claimed by Portugal. It's called São Tomé."

I held my breath.

"It's said to be filled with giant lizards, snakes, and other venomous monsters." He grimaced with amused eyes. "People never lived on the island because it has a deadly fever that kills most who get it." He waved his hand in the air. "Only the strongest survive."

Enjoying the tension he created, the traveler lowered his voice as if confiding a secret. "King Joao decided to settle São Tomé- but he didn't want to risk the lives of God-fearing Christians. He came up with a great idea. The King is sending the *degradados,* Portugal's worst criminals, who have been jailed or exiled, to colonize São Tomé. You know, *assassinos e ladroes,* murderers and thieves . . ."

The traveler's eyes danced, savoring the attention. "Ah, yes," he rubbed his nose and spat. "*That* was not enough. The King decided since he owned the Jews, he would send them to São Tomé along with the degradados. He didn't want his colony to be filled with Christ-killers so his majesty decreed that all Jewish children, between the ages of two to fourteen, should be taken from their families, shipped to the island, and raised as Christians."

The traveler slapped his knee and laughed.

3

Our secret hideout with Aldonca and Goncallo didn't feel safe anymore.

"We'll protect you," the old couple insisted.

I wondered how two old peasants could possibly protect us from the King's soldiers but I didn't say anything.

The next day an aging merchant arrived with more news about the King. The merchant patted his belly and stuffed his mouth with olives as he described how merciless soldiers ripped babies and children from their parents' arms.

"Women throw themselves at the King's feet begging to be allowed to go with their children," he smiled with stained, broken teeth. "I saw it with my own eyes. Old men tore their beards when children are seized. If anyone fights, the soldiers start the beatings, often killing them. And the crying! *Meu Deus*, the wail of babies reaching for their mamas' tits as soldiers wrench them off is horrible."

The merchant smirked. "Christ-killers. They deserve it."

It was a horror greater than any of us could imagine. I remembered the children living in the streets with their parents; I heard their screams and saw their eyes frozen in terror. King Joao II was more heartless than Ferdinand and Isabella, equal only to the ruthless Torquemada.

The countryside turned dark; threats lurked behind every tree. Would the soldiers find us? We huddled, terrified by the latest change in our world. Aldonca and Goncallo tried to reassure us but we knew they would be helpless against the soldiers.

The truth was harsh. King Joao II was our enemy not our savior! We fled Spain only to confront a new, perhaps worse danger. I started to sniff the air for dust from galloping horses and press my ear against the ground for the rumble of their hooves. We tried not to talk about it but the idea of kidnapped Jewish children was terrifying. At sixteen, Hanna was too old . . . but me? What would happen if they found me?

A young, pleasant-faced traveler from Lisboa stopped on his way to better fortune in Spain. He sat on a rock outside of the hut and told us he was seeking adventure far from the stink of Lisboa. He sipped water, smiled and warned us of soldiers in the countryside searching for hidden Jewish children. He left, rubbing his thumb and forefinger together as if expecting coin.

My hamsa got warm. I touched it and the charm throbbed as if trying to tell me something. I watched the pleasant-faced traveler until I couldn't see him anymore. We went back to our chores but my hamsa remained warm. What was it saying? I heard Mama's voice in my head.

He's going to betray you.

It didn't make any sense. I paused and watched the others. They didn't hear Mama's voice.

Betrayed.

"They're coming for us," I cried. "The traveler sold his information."

The others laughed nervously.

"It's your imagination," Aldonca patted my back.

"It's not my imagination."

Hanna stared at me.

"My hamsa and Mama are warning me . . ."

No one knew what to do.

Goncallo pressed his ear to the ground. "I hear something."

"What?"

"We have to hide," Hanna screamed.

Suddenly I heard them too – along with rising dust and the sound of horses' hooves. There were no trapdoors or tunnels – no place to go.

"Hide!" Aldonca cried. "Follow me."

Goncallo grabbed their only cow, a large creature with dark, soulful eyes. We raced into the barn but this time we went into the cow's stall. Aldonca furiously dug a hole in the straw. We crawled in and she covered us. Goncallo moved the cow into the stall; there was barely room between us and the cow's hooves.

"Quiet," Aldonca warned.

"Yes."

"*Deus ajuda-nos,*" she added. God help us.

I curled next to Hanna and didn't move. I peered outside between the straw and the cow's hooves. Aldonca and Goncallo pretended to do chores. My world shifted into blinding red. This was the second time I felt such terror . . . the first was when Mama shoved me through the trapdoor in Spain. Hanna and I trembled like animals caught in a trap, our enemy upon us. I prayed.

Shema Yisrael Adonai Elohaenu Adonai Echad

The words were said silently, only my lips moved.

Will God hear me?

The soldiers appeared at the edge of the clearing. There were five of them, each rode a heavy, stomping horse. They wore red

Christian crosses on their gray tunics, fearsome helmets, and carried razor-sharp swords. One soldier held a little girl with tangled, curly black hair, draped across his saddle like a sack of grain.

They spoke. Gruff male voices in difficult-to-understand Portuguese.

"Where is the Jewish child?"

"There is no child here," Goncallo lowered his head. "It is only two poor old people."

"We *know* there's a Jewish child. A traveler told us."

"There are no travelers here. We are too poor . . ."

One of the soldiers spurred his horse close to Goncallo and kicked the old man's head. Goncallo's legs buckled and he tumbled to the ground.

The others laughed as Aldonca screamed and ran to his side, gathering the old man in her arms.

The soldier dismounted and kicked Goncallo again, smashing the old man's head and ribs while he raised his hands in glee.

"By decree of His Most Catholic Majesty, King Joao II," the soldier roared, "all Jews between two and fourteen years are to be removed from their homes and sent to the Holy See of Africa to receive baptism and redemption in the faith of Our Lord Christ Jesus."

I held my breath and watched from beneath the straw.

Aldonca and Goncallo were silent.

"Jew lovers," one soldier mumbled. "We should kill you."

"Hey," the other soldier pointed to the hut. "The King only wants the kids."

"Yeah. Let's move it."

Shaking their heads, two soldiers dismounted and entered the hut. They smashed the few precious pieces of Aldonca's pottery. They quickly emerged – the old couple didn't have much.

"No Jewish swine," one grumbled.

"Check out the barn, Simao."

The soldier who had brutalized Goncallo nodded. With a final sweep, Simao kicked Goncallo on the back of his neck and began his search for Jewish children.

Goncallo didn't move.

The dark-haired child held on the saddle stirred. She began to cry. "Quiet," the soldier slapped her, "or I'll feed you to the pigs."

She was still.

The soldier named Simao swaggered across the clearing and entered the barn. He poked through the donkey's empty stall. Then he paused and stared at the cow.

4

The scream rose in my throat.

Bugs scurried across my arms, leaving tiny bites in their wake. Sweat beaded on my forehead as if death hovered a few steps away.

"Stay still," Hanna whispered.

Stay still? How can I stay still when my heart pounded and my mind burned with fire?

"Stay still or it's over."

The world moved in crazy, dizzying waves. My nose filled with the acrid scent of fear. I saw red – the color of my blood. Our blood. Sparkling in the summer sun beneath a cloudless sky.

I heard *him* move closer. No face just boot-steps. Moving closer and closer until he paused in front of me and called to the other soldiers. I could see his piercing blue eyes and caramel-colored hair between the straw.

"I think I found something."

There was laughter. "What have you found, Simao? Gold?"

More laughter.

I closed my eyes and pretended that there was no Simao, no gold, and no mound of straw that hid me and Hanna from the soldiers. We were home and Mama was cooking dinner and Papa was coming from business. Maybe I'll see my best friends Isabel and Palos tomorrow. We'll wear our crosses and sneer at Jews who don't hide themselves.

"Marranos," Isabel would spat.

Palos would wave his arms and make ugly noises.

Isabel never knew the truth until we fled. Isabel thought her best friends were Catholic, devoutly praying to the Lord Jesus Christ. Not heretics and the cursed messengers of Satan.

Palos was one of us, a Secret Jew who lived by the Laws of Moses. We saw each other sometimes in the tunnels and rooms. He would smile shyly. Isabel never knew. It was our secret.

There was no time to remember. If Simao turned his back and forgot his search – if there was a miracle and God protected us – we could think and talk . . .

Simao didn't like his friends making fun of him. I heard his breathing quicken, felt his anger rise like steam from a cooking pot.

"You haven't found any children here," Simao retorted. "Maybe I will."

There was laughter. Sharp, ugly sounds. "We have one already, Simao. From the other farm. Now it's your turn."

"I'll find one – a real Jew baby," Simao growled.

An icy sweat swaddled my body. Hanna shivered next to me. I'm still young . . . but she is full-grown at sixteen years. What will the soldiers do with her?

"Simao's gold," the soldiers taunted him.

I smelled his rage.

Hanna gripped my hand so tightly it hurt.

Time slowed as Simao bent over the straw. I see him in my mind's eye – a brutal Portuguese soldier searching for children, hungry for spoils. Stinking and unwashed. Rotted teeth and putrid breath so close that I could smell his lust.

Simao slowly parted the straw that hid us.

5

I'll never forget his hands. His thick, short fingers were calloused from hard labor; faint red scars crisscrossed the palms and tuffs of short, wiry hair curled like stains at the base of each finger. His hands stopped time. We were in a world without sound or movement – just fingers plucking at our souls. We prayed the fingers would be satisfied – miraculously retreat like an army that's savaged its enemy and ready to return home.

Mama please.

God please.

Help us.

Simao pushed away the straw. Dirty, caramel-colored hair fell over hard, icy blue eyes. He stared at us. "I found something," he hissed.

There was laughter from the other soldiers. "And what have you found, Simao?"

Time froze as Simao stared.

He licked his lips.

6

I stared into his eyes. They were an icy, snakelike blue. A hideous smile slithered across his face.

"Look what I found," he cried joyfully. "I got me a Jewish baby and a Jewish *puta.* Whore. We can take the baby and fuck the whore."

There was a chorus of cheers from the soldiers outside.

We had gone through so much since The Inquisitors came to our home. Hanna had been brave, took good care of me, and faced the unknown. Now she trembled violently.

Simao licked his lips and tossed away the straw. "Ah yes," he hissed, "we have us a Jewish whore."

He wrenched me and Hanna to our feet. Hanna's olive skin turned pale, her eyes filled with terror. He grabbed at her breasts.

She pulled away and covered herself with her arms. Simao dragged us into the open beneath cheers from the soldiers.

"Take the Jew whore," the one in the saddle shouted, "but leave the baby clean."

"*Puta*," Simao grinned.

"I'm not a baby," I stepped in front of Hanna. "Leave her alone."

The soldiers roared.

"Maybe you're not a baby," Simao reached for my privates, "but we need a Jew kid. You work. She doesn't. That makes her mine."

"She's not . . ."

Simao grabbed me like a sack of grain and tossed me onto a saddle. Another soldier pinned me down.

"Hold her for me," he said, tossing the reins to one of the soldiers on foot. "We'll take turns with the other."

I fought and screamed. Simao grinned and beat me across my shoulders.

"No blood," another advised.

"You're right," Simao backed away.

Suddenly Hanna lunged at him from behind, hanging on his back and scratching his face with her nails.

"Can't control a whore," the soldier who pinned me laughed.

Simao's eyes burned with rage. He flung Hanna off him as if she were a bug. Their eyes locked. "Take care of the baby." Simao growled.

I screamed, fighting to be free of the soldier's hands.

"Keep her quiet," Simao snarled.

The soldier punched me hard on my head. I was stunned. He held onto my clothes so I wouldn't slide off the saddle. The world turned black.

"Take her," the soldier said pointing to Simao. "You first."

Me? Then I realized what was going to happen. I forced myself into consciousness. "No," I cried but no one cared. The soldier slapped me again.

"Don't move or I'll kill you," he said.

I was helpless.

"Good girl. He forced me to sit up. "We can't take you but we'll have the other. And you'll learn what men do to Jewish whores."

He held me tight so I couldn't move.

"Make sure the baby *sees*," Simao called over his shoulder. Another set of hands grabbed my face and forced my eyelids open.

Simao circled Hanna. She lunged at him again, her hands clawing at his face. "Fucking puta," he mumbled. He caught her arms and twisted her body until she fell to the ground. He held her immobilized with one knee. She fought him beating with her fists but it only made him laugh. He leaned over and pinned her arms beneath her body.

Hanna couldn't move.

He ripped off her clothes. He pulled out his private, which was stiff and hard, and rubbed it against her. Hanna screamed. The louder she got the more he enjoyed it.

"I'm going to fuck you," he snarled. "Fight me Jewish puta and I'll kill you."

Hanna struggled wildly.

He slapped her across the face. "Whore," he cried gleefully.

He grabbed her throat. "Fight me and I'll kill you. I'm going to fuck you dead or alive."

In the distance I heard the soldiers cheering him. Hanna bit his neck and drew blood but he didn't care. "I'm going to fuck you like you've never been fucked before," he hissed. "And when I finish, you know what you're going to say my Jewish *puta*? Thank you. Thank you. Thank you." He laughed maniacally.

The soldiers cheered louder.

Simao forced Hanna's legs apart. His breath was so loud it sounded like a raging wind.

"No," I cried again. No one cared.

Hanna screamed when Simao bit her bared breasts. She screamed when he entered her, ripping apart her insides. He beat her face. "Shut up *puta*," he roared.

He thrust harder and harder, grunting like an animal. The soldiers shouted their approval. With a howl that sent spittle over Hanna's face, he finished.

Beaming, Simao stood up. He tucked away his privates and surveyed Hanna. Then he stepped back. "She's yours," he waved his fist in the air.

The soldiers took turns. Each one thrusting and grunting until he was finished. Winking at me, knowing that I was forced to watch. I was sick and furious and terrified. But they held my head and forced my eyelids open so I wouldn't miss anything. It wasn't Hanna's screams that broke my heart – it was her silence.

They soldiers returned to their horses when they finished. Hanna lay naked and numb and twisted.

"Hanna," I cried out to her.

She didn't respond. The soldiers chuckled.

Simao surveyed his work. "The whore got what she deserved."

The soldiers agreed.

"You're headed for São Tomé Jew girl," he said as he climbed on the horse. I smelled his sex pressed against my back.

"Noooooooo!" I wailed. "Nooooooo!"

But Hanna was broken and Aldonca and Goncallo crushed in the dirt. I cried to the sky; I cried to God; I cried to Mama and Papa. No one heard.

It was the last time I saw Hanna.

Tama

1

The wind tore at my face as I clung to the rough, scratchy brown mane of Simao's horse. I was his prize. He defiled Hanna and took me away. Perhaps he killed her soul? Why didn't I save her? Why didn't I try harder?

I let them rape my sister.

My world had been a nightmare since the day The Inquisitors arrived but I always had Hanna. Now she was gone. What would happen to her? What would happen to me?

I struggled not to be sick. I fought the questions and images of Hanna being raped. And then I heard Papa's decree.

Live and continue the seed of our family.

How can I, Papa? Without Hanna?

What was next? Where was I going? What was São Tomé? Was I broken by Kings who hated Jews if they didn't convert?

The forces were too powerful – they always won. Without Mama, Papa, and Hanna, I was doomed. I struggled to understand the dizzying politics – make some order of questions without answers. I couldn't comprehend why anyone would hate a person because of their belief in the Laws of Moses. Didn't Papa teach us that we held true to our birthright that went back thousands of years? Wasn't Jesus born Jewish? Wasn't it a *good* thing?

The questions would never be answered. They were my past, my present, and my future. My job now was to stay alive. Honor Mama, Papa, and Hanna. Simao didn't care if I fell off. I was just another Jew girl used for his purposes. I remembered the word that Isabel used to call the Jews – Marrano – swine. To Simao I was swine, something to be owned, butchered, and devoured. I was a thing not a person.

I wondered what Palos was thinking. Was he talking to Isabel and pretending to be horrified at my true identity?

The Red Cross on Simao's chest was pressed up against my back as we galloped through the countryside with the other four soldiers and the little curly-haired girl. We flew across the land much faster than when Hanna and I walked searching for sanctuary. Simao was a stone wall, hard and unyielding against me. I tried not to tremble but he felt like fire searing my skin. Hanna's screams reverberated through my mind, tearing my heart into shreds. I should have helped her. I should have stopped them. I had a forever picture of her being gang raped, her screams dying as they leaped on her laughing and grunting and taking their fill. I felt her pain and humiliation; saw their hard, purple privates attacking her, their bodies sweating and shuddering between her legs. I heard their climaxes like battle cries, screaming their victory. What kind of victory was it to rape a beautiful Jewish girl?

Why didn't I stop it?

The worst picture was the last – Hanna lying still, defiled, and Aldonca clawing the dirt to reach her. Maybe they'll take care of Hanna – nurse her back to life? Was that possible – or had the soldiers killed her spirit? Everyone I loved had been left behind me. I cried out but each time I made a sound Simao slapped my head.

It hurt and I didn't want to hurt anymore.

Simao laughed and hissed and gave me warnings in the wind.

"If you cry you'll end up like your sister."

"If you fight me I'll throw you in the dust."

"If you make me unhappy I'll run my sword through you like a pig on the spit. Then I'll eat you . . . do you know, Jew girl, that the King's soldiers eat little girls for dinner?"

Fear pummeled me. I tried to calm myself by taking stock of where I was. I would never see Mama and Papa again. I would never see Hanna again.

How could I survive without Hanna? She was so smart . . . she knew so much. What did I know? Terror gripped me like Simao's fingers – I trembled inside and remembered when the neighbor's baby, tiny Maria, cried through the night. She screamed and trembled and sweat covered her body. Mama told me she was very sick. The next day I woke up and Mama said that little Maria had died. I asked Mama how that happened – why would a baby die? Mama said that Maria returned to God; she was happy and safe. I didn't believe her. Maria was dead like the people in Lisboa. Dead.

I didn't want to die like Maria and the people in Lisboa. I didn't want to be like them even if God was waiting for me. Papa told me I *had* to live. A scream stuck in my throat. Will God be angry at me because I don't want to be with Him?

I wished that Mama, Papa and Hanna were here to answer my questions. Comfort me. I shook my head. No one could help me anymore. It was up to me, alone. I had to live for them. Maybe if I died I would see them again but I wasn't ready to go to God yet.

My fear transformed into anger. Tears raced down my face but the wind dried them quickly. Suddenly Mama's arms were around me. Her voice was gentle. The horse galloped faster moving further away from everything I ever knew or loved. Mama called out to me.

Be strong my little one. I'm with you.

No! You're not with me, Mama. You're with Papa and the Inquisitors in a dungeon . . . Hanna is on the ground . . .

And then I felt it. The hamsa. Mama's hamsa. It was warm against my skin. I touched it and knew that I wasn't completely alone.

Simao felt me squirm. He laughed and smacked my head. I felt dizzy like I might fall off the horse. I held on tighter, my heart pounding wildly.

"Watch it," Simao warned, "or you'll end up like your sister. Puta." He laughed, his voice eaten by the wind. "Good meat, I would have her again any day. A virgin! Since little red-headed sister is here maybe I should prepare for dinner . . ."

I shivered. Will Simao and the soldiers do to me what they did to Hanna? Or Mama? Simao was hungry. He didn't care. He could stop the horse, throw me to the ground . . . The soldiers' words came back.

Take the Jew whore, Simao, but leave the baby clean.

Maybe you're not a baby," Simao retorted, "but we need a Jew kid. You work.

She doesn't."

I won't let them win. The voices of my ancestors raced through thousands of years, crossing the Red Sea, fleeing the Egyptians, surviving the massacres and pogroms. I had their blood.

I had to survive.

2

Simao slowed his mount. He pointed to a stream and guided his horse to the edge. He leaped off the saddle, the Red Cross on his chest gleaming in the sun.

"Don't move," he warned, "or I'll fuck you like your sister."

He coaxed his horse to drink. The other soldiers dismounted. As the animals noisily slurped water, I watched the curly-headed little girl. She was on the horse next to me. Simao and the soldiers waded into the water to drink. They couldn't hear me speak to the girl.

"Hi."

She stiffened and sat upright. Even then I could see how tiny she was – no older than five years. Her brown eyes were wide with fear, her lips trembled, and her hair was tangled and dirty. She looked at me but didn't speak.

"I'm Esperanza. What's your name?"

The little girl blinked but didn't respond.

"I'm scared too."

A faint smile played across her lips.

"Can you speak?"

The little girl glanced at the soldiers.

"Let's be friends. We both need friends now."

Silence.

"I lost my big sister. You can be like my little sister. I'll take care of you like Hanna took care of me."

"Shut up," Simao ordered. He stood between me and the little girl. "No talking."

"She didn't talk . . ." I began but he slapped my leg. "I do the talking," he hissed. He threw his leg up and heaved himself back in the saddle.

"Hey Simao," another soldier called. "You like young meat? You can take the baby here – like her sister – if you want. We'll watch."

Simao cursed in Portuguese and slid away from me.

He kicked the horse and we were off again, racing ahead of the others through the countryside.

It was nearly dark when we stopped again. Simao followed the other soldiers into a large courtyard. There were two stone-and-wood warehouses with heavy wooden doors. Monks, nuns, priests, and soldiers milled around hundreds of children, from infants to older than me. Some of them looked very angry, others sad, their cheeks stained with tears. A few had blank faces as if they felt nothing. Simao dismounted and yanked me from the saddle.

"I should have taken you when I had the chance," he hissed and spewed rancid breath. The other soldier roughly dropped the little girl to the ground. A monk, dressed in heavy brown robes came immediately.

"Bless you," the monk said to the soldiers. "You have honored the will of your King as well as our Lord, Jesus Christ."

The soldiers nodded as the monk grabbed our arms. Simao gave me one last hungry look and returned to the saddle.

The monk smelled of sweat and greasy food.

"Two girls, eh?"

He dragged us to a large group of children. I was afraid to look into his eyes. They were tiny beads peering from beneath his hooded robe.

"The girls go here," he indicated the building on the left, "and the boys to the right. No talking."

The little girl grabbed my hand.

"What's your name?" I asked gently.

She looked at me silently.

"I won't hurt you."

She pleaded with her eyes.

"If you don't tell me your name, I'll have to give you one."

She shook her head and threw her arms around me, hugging tightly.

"OK. You must have a name. I'll call you Tama, or the innocent one."

The little girl smiled weakly.

"Enough," the monk roared. "Didn't you hear what I said? Girls to the left, boys to the right. No talking or I'll beat you."

I pulled Tama away from me and took her hand. "We'll stick together."

The monk shoved us. Another monk emerged from the shadows. He was short with a gentle voice. "Here," he said and led us to the left.

"Stay with me, Tama. I'll take care of you." I whispered.

We were not alone. I saw sisters and friends, neighbors and strangers, holding on to one another as the monks directed them. Boys to the right. Girls to the left. Some of the boys looked older than fourteen. Some of the girls clutched babies in their arms. Why would the soldiers steal babies? The girls tried to comfort the infants but they cried for their mama's breasts, filling the air with their wails.

Then everyone began to cry.

The noise was horrible – the babies' wails, children's cries and smell of fear. The monks tried to quiet the kids – slapping the older children, shoving the little ones. To no avail. The cries increased as if reaching into heaven. Maybe God would hear us?

We crossed the plaza sobbing beneath the searing eyes of the adults. They moved us left to the cavernous stone warehouse that housed the girls.

Tama shivered as we were thrust inside. It was hideous – a cold, dark, filthy space bursting with stolen children and reeking from the rotten food it usually stored. Rats scurried in the shadows. Monks and nuns milled through the throngs, handing out pieces of bread, offering water and making no attempt to soothe the terrified children. Some children ate hungrily, others stared, too frightened to do anything. Many of the older girls prayed but if they were caught, the monks or nuns smacked their faces, leaving fingerprints on their cheeks.

"No Hebrew or Ladino," the monks ordered, "it's the language of Satan. From now on you will be beaten if we hear you speaking that tongue. Sit against the wall and don't move."

We found a small spot in the corner and sat obediently. The last group of girls entered the warehouse followed by nuns in black habits with white swaths of cloth covering their heads and necks and long heavy black veils. The girls cowered, whether alone, with a companion, or in a small group. They shrank against the stone wall, not daring to speak.

The monks and nuns watched and waited, impatiently tapping their feet or rubbing their hands.

"Quickly, quickly," they demanded.

When everyone was settled a miserable silence permeated the warehouse – as cold and harsh as the stone walls. A fat monk – apparently the leader – stood up in the middle of the warehouse. He scanned the girls, his eyes boring into each child's face. Then he cleared his throat, rubbed his nose and sighed in disgust. His voice echoed in the stone building, bouncing off the walls like a message from God.

"You are now the possessions of King Joao."

3

The monk took a deep breath and smiled. He lowered his head as if commencing a prayer.

"King Joao *owns* you. All of you. As Jews, you are the children of Satan. The same Jews who murdered our Lord and Savior Jesus Christ. But our King is merciful and we forgive you for being born with evil in your souls. King Joao has taken you from the vile grasp of your parents and thus saved you from eternity in hell. God Bless our royal majesty, King Joao II."

Save me? Mama, Papa, Hanna – were they saved by this monk's God? Or protected by mine? What did King Joao do for *them*?

"In that spirit," the monk continued, "you will speak no Ladino – say no Hebrew Prayers." The monk's eyes glowed with the fire of his faith. "They are the words of your parents and you parent's parents. Satan is in their souls. We will change that forever. We will baptize you with the love of God." He grinned. "By the mercy of our Lord Jesus Christ, you will obey the one true faith."

My blood turned to ice. Strange words were chanted. The nuns and monks crossed themselves. Several priests circled around us and sprinkled water on our heads.

"No," an older girl cried. Her light brown hair flew in all directions, her eyes went wild. She stood up, waving her arms. "Don't you see what they're doing? They're baptizing us. Don't let them. You *can't* let them." Her voice rang out. Softly, a few other girls followed her lead.

Shema Yisrael Adonai Elohaenu Adonai Echad.

They enraged the monk. He leaped across the space, kicking a group of young children out of his way. He grabbed the girl by the hair and dragged her into the center of the warehouse where we could all watch her punishment.

"Speak the language of Lucifer," he roared, "and watch what happens to sinners." She tried to sit up but he kicked her in the belly. "Devil, devil," he chanted as he beat her with his fist, screaming Portuguese words I didn't understand. He broke her nose, spattering blood in all directions. She lowered her head and tried to protect herself. The monk kicked her in the head and she fell flat, not moving.

"You are now Christian," the monk bellowed, spittle dripping from his mouth and down his chin. He kicked the girl's still body. "All of you received the Beneficence of Conversion and Redemption in The Catholic Faith of Our Lord Christ Jesus. If I hear any of you speaking the words of the devil, you will be beaten. If we catch you carrying any of the artifacts of the devil, you will be beaten. We must protect your souls for your own good!"

We were afraid to move. Tama held on to me tightly.

"Heretics," two nuns chanted. "Heretics, heretics, heretics."

The monk wiped the girl's blood off his hands and onto his robe. "If you persist," he threatened in a low voice like a dog growling, "you'll be thrown into the water when we reach the sea or thrown to the lizards when we reach São Tomé. You'll spend eternity in the fires of hell."

Tama and I trembled. We believed the monk. We didn't know what sin we had committed to deserve the fires of hell but it didn't matter. We knew what the punishment was.

I hugged Tama. "We'll be okay," I lied. "I promise."

I didn't know if I could keep my promise.

Tama and I huddled closer, quivering with cold and fear. A girl next to us watched.

"My name is Rosada," she said flatly. "If you think this is bad . . . well I know where we're going."

"I do too."

"São Tomé."

I nodded.

"Do you know what São Tomé *is*?" Rosada asked, her cheeks bright red.

"An island?"

Rosada laughed like a mad woman. "It's an island where giant lizards eat children!"

"No."

"Yes. We're all going to die – the lizards will have us for dinner."

"Not true."

"Is."

"No."

I turned my back and tried not to listen to the crazy cackles of Rosada's laughter. I knew I would never sleep . . . but my eyes closed and I cuddled Tama and the cold stone wall.

I dreamed about Hanna.

4

I woke to the chanting of nuns and monks.

Glory be to the Father, and to the Son, and to the Holy Spirit;
As it was in the beginning, is now, and will be for ever. Amen.

My back ached from sleeping against the stone and supporting Tama. I was chilled all over. For a moment I forgot where I was – my head said I was home, waiting for Mama to wake me up, tell me my chores for the day, giggle with Hanna, smell food cooking . . . my eyes and ears told me something very different.

All-powerful God, help us to proclaim the power of the Lord's resurrection.

The words penetrated my thoughts. Present returned.

May we who accept the sign of the love of Christ come to share the eternal life he reveals.

Everything came back . . . Aldonca and Goncallo trying to protect us, Goncallo collapsing in the dust; Hanna lying in the dirt. Simao laughing, fondling my privates. I saw the other soldiers, their privates plunged into Hanna as they grunted and sweated like pigs. Lastly, I heard Hanna's cries and worse, her silence.

I shook my head to scatter the images.

I touched Tama's shoulder to make sure she was there and I wasn't totally alone.

For he lives and reigns with you and the Holy Spirit, one God, for ever and ever.

"I'm a Jew!" I wanted to scream it out loud but it was only a whimper. I thought of the light-haired girl and the monk's warning that the girls would be beaten if anyone spoke Hebrew. I said the *Shema* under my breath so no one would hear.

Shema Yisrael Adonai Elohaenu Adonai Echad.

Hanna had told me these were dangerous times and I had to be very careful.

"Think before you speak, Esperanza. Don't do anything crazy because you don't know what people will do. Even good people."

I don't understand . . . people hated *Conversos* so much they took Mama and Papa from us. People hated Jews so much they took me from Aldonca and Goncallo who *were* Christians, and Hanna . . .

I shook my head. It made no sense. If the love of Christ was so powerful, why did the monks have to beat children? Why did the King have to kidnap me? Why would their God let soldiers batter gentle Aldonca and Goncallo and a monk beat the light-haired girl?

"Novos Christaos," a monk thrust bread into my hands. "Eat for your strength and God's gift."

Our eyes met. His were gentle but glazed with a kindness sheathed in ice. I took a deep breath and nibbled on the bread. I wasn't hungry. I was tired and hurt and dreaded what would happen next.

I looked for Rosada but she was gone. I was relieved. Her talk about giant lizards that ate children was too scary. I wanted Tama to be brave. She had slept fitfully, her tiny arms thrashed at the air. She called out for someone – a baby crying for her Mama? I wondered how much Tama would remember years from now. Would she be able to see her mama? Hear her voice? I sighed, split my bread in half and tried to wake her very gently. Tama needed food. Instead, she opened her eyes and started screaming, her arms and legs flailing the air.

"Silence!" A nun ordered.

"We'll beat her into quiet," a fat monk added, "if we have to."

No! I couldn't let that happen to Tama. I pulled her into my arms and held her like Hanna did to me in the straw. I covered her mouth with my fingers so everyone thought she was calm. Tama trembled so badly it felt like she would break into a thousand pieces. I sang softly so the monks wouldn't hear – one of Mama's lullabies in Ladino.

Durme, durme mi alma donzeya
Sleep, sleep my beautiful child

Durme, durme sin ansia i dolor
Sleep without worry or sorrow.

It worked. Tama's body relaxed and her arms and legs stilled as she listened to me. I fed her tiny pieces of bread but she could only eat a few mouthfuls.

"Can you talk now, Tama?"

Her dark eyes widened in fear.

I stroked her tangled, curly dark hair trying to smooth it with my fingers. "It's okay – I'll talk for both of us. You're safe, Tama, I won't let anyone hurt you. You'll talk when you're ready."

Tama shook her head and peered around the warehouse. Some girls wandered aimlessly, mumbling under their breaths. Others were still eating their bread, watching and waiting. Still others were motionless; their bodies sprawled like half-empty sacks of grain.

"*Morto.*" I heard the nuns whisper.

"Get the boys."

Within minutes a skinny, scowling monk appeared leading a group of older boys into the warehouse. I knew that the King only wanted Jewish children between ages two and fourteen. The boys looked older. Fifteen or sixteen? They were tall with strong shoulders and long legs.

The girls that carried babies in their arms also looked older.

What were *they* doing here?

"Bring them outside," a monk pointed to the motionless children.

One boy passed in front of me, his eyes full of rage. "They're dead," he snarled. "They're the lucky ones."

My heart pounded as the boys picked up a little dead girl near us.

Why did she die? Had she given up? Did God call her into heaven?

I watched the boys work in a grim procession. Suddenly I saw the light-haired girl that the monk had beaten when she said the Shema. Her face was caked in dried blood, her body twisted into an impossible position. The monk – the representative of Jesus Christ – had murdered her.

"Is she in the eternal fires of hell or next to God?" I asked a nearby nun.

The nun pretended not to hear. Tama shivered.

"We're not going to die!" I cried defiantly. "I'm not going to let that happen."

The nun smiled. She stood over me and looked into my eyes, her habit flowing in dark waves. "No, little one, you're now in the hands of our Lord, Jesus Christ. He won't let you die."

"He let them die."

She shook her head. "We can never fully understand the ways of the Lord."

Her voice was so soft I wanted to ask her to take me back to Hanna, Aldonca, and Goncallo. I wanted to tell her that I'm afraid to go to a strange island where lizards eat children. I wanted to tell her so many things . . . but her eyes burned with the same religious fire that I saw in the monks. I knew that she believed Jews were emissaries of Satan; Christ-killers and heretics.

She was gone before I could muster the courage to say anything.

"I won't let us die," I repeated more to myself than Tama.

Tama's eyes fluttered. I wondered if she heard or even understood what I said. Maybe that was better. Tama didn't need to understand.

After the dead children were removed, the scowling monk left with the boys. The girls were very quiet, finally understanding that we were caught in some awful spider's web – tiny insects with no way out.

The fiery monk from last night appeared, followed by a helmeted soldier. I turned away as they stood before us in the center of the warehouse. He raised his arms and demanded our attention. The soldier raised his sword.

"Novos Christaos," the monk shouted, "children of our Lord Jesus Christ, hear ye." He paused. "Listen carefully and don't move or you'll be beaten."

The soldier stepped forward and removed his helmet. He was very ugly with icy snakelike blue eyes, dirty caramel-colored hair, and rotted teeth. Tama's mouth opened in a silent scream. I couldn't breathe.

Simao.

"By Righteous Decree of His Most Catholic Majesty, King Joao II," Simao bellowed, "all Jewish children, male and female, between two and fourteen years of age are exiled and shall be transported to the Holy See of Africa. You have already received baptism and are now the children of Our Lord, Jesus Christ. You will join the *degradados* under the leadership of Alvaro de Caminha, *Donatario da Ilha de São Tomé,* to work and live in the colony of São Tomé."

Simao smirked.

I didn't know whether to be more afraid of Simao or São Tomé.

"São Tomé," one girl started to cry. Others joined her until the warehouse echoed with sobbing children. Rosado's words rang in my ears.

São Tomé is an island where giant lizards eat children for dinner.

Our shipmates would be *assassinos e ladroes*, Portuguese murderers and thieves.

And Alvaro de Caminha.

How would we survive? How could I possibly protect me and Tama?

"We'll make it," I lied to Tama.

She turned her face away.

The nuns and monks got very busy. They made the girls stand, slapping them if they cried.

"*Silencio.*"

The girls had to move away from the wall as the nuns searched them, making sure that no one carried anything Jewish. I held my breath when the soft-voiced num approached me.

"You look like a good Christian girl," she muttered as she touched me. Her hands slid over my body and stopped at Mama's hamsa. Our eyes met.

"Your mama's charm?"

I nodded. "Please, it's the only thing I have . . ."

"You have nothing. You're a good Christian girl now." She smiled and moved to the next girl.

I kept my hamsa. Maybe Mama *was* watching over me?

When the search was complete they formed us into lines and led us outside. The open plaza was ablaze in bright sun. There were no clouds in the sky. The boys were already there, closely guarded by a line of monks and soldiers. Anyone out of line was beaten. A few boys tried to run. The monks quickly caught them, thrashing their backs and shoulders with switches used for donkeys. The boys cringed and cried out but the monks were merciless. Many fell to the ground beneath the monk's punishments – some stood shakily, faces streaked in blood.

"Listen to us," one monk sneered, "or you'll be beaten like the swine you come from."

"Stay quiet," I whispered to Tama. "Just do what they say."

Tama turned her dark eyes to mine. She didn't speak but I knew she understood.

More monks and nuns arrived until we were completely surrounded by a wall of robes and habits. Beyond the line of clerics were the soldiers sporting red crosses and swords. I knew that one of them was Simao but I had lost track of him in the mob.

Why did they need so many adults to control children?

The two groups formed a procession. At the head was the fiery monk and Simao. For an instant, Simao turned and our eyes met. Before I could look away, he grinned and licked his lips.

Sao Gabriel

1

It was said that the Portuguese carracks were the best ships in the world. They traveled long distances and handled rough seas with grace. The carracks were stronger, roomier and more resilient. None of the children had ever been aboard a carrack.

We were headed for the docks.

I looked up into the sky. A bird watched, as if waiting for carrion.

The soldiers, nuns, and monks herded us to the docks at Lisboa port. They tried to keep us calm, forming a human wall as we approached the harbor plaza. In the beginning it was peaceful, almost pretty. We saw the carracks bobbing in the water, their masts towering over everything.

"We're going on the *Sao Gabriel,*" someone said. Within minutes everyone knew.

"Our ship is named for an angel," I poked Tama. "Gabriel. That's a good omen. Gabriel was the archangel known as God's messenger. The Christians called him a saint. The Moors believed he revealed the Koran to Muhammad. That means he likes *all* people."

The nuns pressed us into a tighter group. We entered the harbor plaza. The girls were followed by the boys. The sky was clear with pigeons on the ground and gulls swooping over our heads. My seagull in the sky seemed to follow us – his squawks drowned out by crazed, screaming throngs of parents swarming the waterfront. There were ear-splitting wails, frantic calls, arms reaching between guards, and people desperately fighting to get closer to their children. All they wanted was to rescue their children from the soldiers, nuns and monks, bring babies back to mama's breasts or have one final embrace. The soldiers, with huge, muscle bound bodies and fierce weapons struggled to contain the parents. The red crosses on their chests reflected the sun like blood, challenging anyone who ventured close. They barely held the parents back.

"Jews! Slaves," one soldier roared. I squinted my eyes in the sun to see if it was Simao.

It was.

"Kill them," Simao howled.

I couldn't stop myself. I charged.

Hands grabbed my arms, shoulders and waist. A monk cursed me, slapping my face so hard that blood spurted from my nose. I didn't care. I wanted to kill Simao – take revenge for Hanna. A nun grabbed my hair and beat me across my shoulders with a donkey whip. I didn't feel anything except rage for Simao. My world turned red as I charged the soldiers who surrounded the girls.

Suddenly there was a scream – not from the parents but from behind me.

"You promised, Esperanza. You promised to take care of me."

They were her first words since we met at Aldonca and Goncallo's hut. I turned to Tama. Her face was filled with terror. "I need you," she whispered.

My rage withered. I had to take care of Tama. It was more important than getting revenge for Hanna. The living had to come first. The nuns and monks thought I retreated because of their beating. My whole body hurt but it didn't matter. I had to take care of Tama.

Tama leaped into my arms.

"I'm sorry. I'm so sorry." Tears mingled with the blood from my broken nose.

Tama nodded, not saying anything. I looked over her head and saw Simao watching us. He grinned and rubbed his privates.

"Move swine," a monk snarled, "or I'll throw you to the soldiers."

Tama and I melted back into the procession. We watched as soldiers got angry and attacked the parents. If one parent broke through their line, the soldiers sent them bleeding and unconscious to the ground. They pounded arms reaching wildly for children and slashed parents with their swords, immune to blood and pain.

The children screamed – their yells pierced the air. Others tried to break away, reaching for mamas and papas. Soldiers, monks and nuns grabbed and twisted those arms until the children yelped in pain. Adult commands fell on deaf ears. Some children, dead or unconscious, were tossed to the side. Later they would be collected by heartbroken parents.

A few parents tossed travel bundles over the heads of the soldiers and between their swords. Children caught the bundles only to have their few possessions seized by soldiers.

I held on to Tama, closed my eyes and tried to block it out.

A fat monk shoved me out of his way. Tama's pleas for mama left her numb and lifeless as if it took everything to say those few words. Across the dock mamas threw themselves at soldier's boots, begging to be allowed to go with their children. Papas prayed, their hands grasping at the air, beseeching God for help. The soldiers kicked them aside and laughed at their desperation.

Suddenly everyone froze. A mother broke through the mob. Simao tried to catch her but she was too fast. She rushed to the children and scooped up her son, a pretty, dark-eyed little boy. Embracing him, she leaped into the water and drowned both of them beneath the hull of a carrack.

For a moment there was stunned silence.

Her husband screamed.

The chaos returned, louder and angrier with cries so frantic that the soldiers cut down unarmed parents like weeds in a field, killing and wounding anyone in their way. Simao stepped forward and recited the words we heard earlier in the warehouse.

By Righteous Decree of His Most Catholic Majesty, King Joao II, all Jewish children, male and female, between two and fourteen years of age are exiled and shall be transported to the Holy See of Africa. They have already received baptism, and are now the children of Our Lord, Jesus Christ. Now they will join the degradados under the leadership of Alvaro de Caminha, to work and live in the colony of São Tomé.

A fresh roar rose from the parents – the soldiers raised their swords. Many parents were killed on the spot. Their children howled in response and monks beat them with donkey switches.

Suddenly Tama became rigid. Her lips trembled. I followed her eyes to a woman trapped behind two soldiers, her arms outstretched. She was screaming something . . . a name . . . that I couldn't hear. No one had to tell me. It was Tama's Mama. For an instant the noise and frenzy muted. There was only Tama and her Mama.

Tama came alive, bawling, arms flailing, blindly fighting her way around a fat nun in a smelly habit.

"Is that your Mama?"

Tama nodded, fighting the monk who plucked her off the ground and held her high like a victory banner.

The woman shrieked. I heard her voice above the others. The monk plunged deeper into the melee with Tama. Separating us. I refused to lose Tama. I waved my arms at Tama's Mama. "I'll take care of her, I promise," I shouted above the noise. For a moment, Tama's Mama stopped struggling. Our eyes met. Her lips moved.

Gracias. May the God of Israel protect you.

Suddenly Simao appeared. He shoved Tama's Mama to the ground and raised his sword, grinning at me. He ran his sword straight through her heart. She lay still on the docks.

I would never tell Tama what I saw.

2

I shoved through the crowd to rescue Tama. The monk tossed her to the ground and I helped her stand. Her face was saturated with tears. We held each other tightly.

"I'll take care of you."

A powerful, angry-looking man with a dark beard and stony face blocked us. He stood like a bronze statue, his dark eyes boring into us. He would not be defied.

Alvaro de Caminha.
Donatario da Ilha de São Tomé.

Our eyes met. When he spoke his voice froze my blood like a chunk of ice thrust into my heart.

Quiet, child.

The Captain of the Sao Gabriel, the Colonial Administrator of São Tomé waved his arms, turned and strode through the crowd.

Tama trembled but was silent.

"Let's go."

We followed the great Alvaro de Caminha, shoving between bodies, tripping over feet and legs and shaking off monks and nuns. I *had* to stay close to the *Donatario*. Whatever our future would bring, I knew it rested in São Tomé with this strange, fierce man.

The noise decreased as we reached the edge of the mob and Alvaro de Caminha paused. He stared at the sight that greeted him – a fleet of three and four-masted carracks bobbing on the water, ready to be boarded. They were beautiful vessels. The ships rose high into the air, their polished wood ready for the sea. The Sao Gabriel was bowl-shaped with a high rear deck, bowed middle and rising front deck. The masts reached into the clouds, covered with unfurled sails and ropes. There were more ropes than I had ever seen in my life. Rope ladders led to the highest point on the ship – a tiny platform called the crow's nest. Sailors dressed in rough, homespun clothes were everywhere. They watched the scene on the dock as if attending a crude; with yellowed teeth, broad smiles, pulsating muscles, and evil glints in their eyes.

I shuddered.

Alvaro de Caminha glanced down at us and realized we had followed him. He snorted.

"That's your home now," he said in an oddly gentle voice. He looked back at the Sao Gabriel, his voice thick with admiration. "It's thirteen hundred leagues to São Tomé. Do you know how long that is?"

"No," I whispered.

"What?" he barked.

"No sir."

He nodded in approval. "It means," he spoke slowly, savoring his words like a mug of fine wine, "that we will be at sea for two months."

He smiled at the shock on my face.

"Many will die. Those who don't behave will be tossed overboard for the sea demons to eat them. Men *and* children. It's not a pretty sight."

My eyes widened in fear. I could hardly breathe.

Alvaro de Caminha threw his head back and laughed so loud that he sprayed me with spittle.

"Do you want to live little one?"

I nodded, unable to speak. Tama hid behind me.

"Then," he bent over slightly as if sharing a secret, "you'll listen to everything the monks tell you. You'll eat your food, send your sickness overboard, and stay quiet and out of the way. If you're good, perhaps you will be saved from the sea demons and the *degradados* who eat little girls like you for dinner." He tilted his head and raised his eyes to the sky. "Of course, pretty girls like you have to watch out for hungry sailors." The Colonial Administrator grinned. "You might be a little girl," he curled his fingers beneath my chin and raised my head to examine my face. "For a hungry sailor with no woman, you can be *his* dinner too."

He laughed at his own wit.

"Red-haired virgins make tasty morsels."

I saw Hanna. In the dirt, soldiers watching. Simao thrusting himself between her legs.

The Colonial Administrator seemed to read my thoughts. "Ah, you know more about men than you let on. He laughed again, slapping his thigh with a thick, broad hand. "Watch your back, pretty little one."

He stood up straight and surveyed the docks. An evil glitter filled his eyes. "Remember, most people say that going to Ilha de São Tomé is a death sentence."

He threw his head back and roared a sound echoing with cruelty. Then he stalked away, laughter drifting behind him like a plume of putrid smoke.

We stood frozen. "We have to fear the sea demons and the degradados, the monks and the sailors," I hissed. "Is there anyone we can trust?"

Tama pulled at her tangled hair.

Once again, she had nothing to say.

3

We watched Alvaro de Caminha's back as he boarded the Sao Gabriel. Two months at sea?

"How are we going to do that?" Tama asked anxiously.

I ran my fingers through my red hair and didn't answer. How could two girls survive that journey? After all we had been through? I glanced at Tama. What had *she* gone through to ultimately end up here on the Lisboa docks? It made no sense – nothing made sense at that moment. The only thing I was sure about was survival – we had to make it to São Tomé. After that we would figure it out.

I had a big job – a promise to fulfill. Papa's words rang in my head.

Live and continue the seed of our family.

Abruptly, the swarm of children shifted. We were engulfed by exhausted cries, glazed eyes, and angry faces. The nuns, monks and soldiers joined forces to push us onto the boat. The sailors watched, licking their lips and wiggling their groins at the older girls. A wail, as if one voice, rose from the parents. We were roughly shoved up the gangplank and onto the ship. The girls, babies, and youngest children were pressed into the rear. We huddled together like kittens in a new litter. I found a spot on the edge where Tama and I could see the docks, the other ships, and the Tagus River beneath. The Tagus flowed into the *Oceano Atlantico* which would take us to Africa.

It was the first time I was on a boat and the first time I would see the ocean.

The boys were separated from the girls by a low wood barrier. We saw them but were warned not to talk or have anything to do with them. The *degradados* were chained to each other in the bow – they looked angry and hungry. I wondered if we should fear them as much as the sea demons, the sailors, and the monks. Although most had purple bruises on their faces and arms, some looked almost *kindly*. Others were bearded and fierce.

Were they just as sad to leave Lisboa?

Alvaro de Caminha's words rang in my ears.

We will be on board for two months.

You will listen to everything the monks tell you.

You will eat your food, send your sickness overboard, and stay quiet and out of way. Perhaps then you will be kept from the sea demons and the degradados *who eat little girls like you for dinner.*

I closed my eyes and Mama's face popped into my mind. She was smiling and told me to be brave, everything would work out. I took a deep breath. I had no choice . . . I had to be brave for Tama. I touched my hamsa praying it would help us.

Tama pulled on my arm and pointed. I opened my eyes and saw the gangplank raised. I heard the final wail of the parents rising like the cries at an *Auto de Fey*. The ropes that secured the ship to the dock were pulled away and slaves on the banks moved us slowly down the river. The people on the dock got smaller, the noise got fainter and Lisboa began to disappear. Small boats with oarsmen took the ropes from the slaves and pulled the Sao Gabriel deeper in the Tagus. Alvaro de Caminha stood high above us and lifted his arms.

"Raise the sails."

A hush fell over the children. There was no turning back. Even the babies were stilled. The degradados sighed and the boys slumped. Tama and I said nothing. There were no more tears left. We held hands tightly and together watched Lisboa fade into the distance until only smoke drifted above the hills and Castelo de Sao Jorge had become history.

4

The time aboard the carrack passed slowly, gradually falling into a routine. We spent our days in the girl's section, sleeping outdoors on the rough planks, and breathing the strange, salty sea air. Tama amused herself by counting small things like crumbs, pebbles, and string. I was impressed that such a young child knew her numbers.

When there was a storm we stayed in the ship's hold. The hatch was closed above us. We slept next to the stable, in complete darkness, drenched in smells of vomit, feces, sickness, and whatever else we imagined. There was a constant chorus of cries – babies and young children were lost without their mamas and papas. The older children were more stalwart, bearing their burdens in the legacy of our Jewish ancestors. Jews knew about exile – it was part of our souls. Many died. Many survived. And many got sick, lingering between life and death as if they didn't know which to choose.

I was determined to obey Papa's command.

Live and continue the seed of our family.

Our family's destiny was up to me.

Tama and I spoke about it in the dark corners of the hold or beneath the stars on the deck. I never knew whether she understood or just listened, soaking in my voice and protection. I became a mama to her – perhaps the hope of her family as well. I thought of her mama, disappearing beneath the soldiers and their Red Crosses and my oath.

I'll take care of her, I promise.

I would take care of Tama even if it meant my death.

When Tama was very sad, I rocked her and sang the lullaby she loved. Tama wasn't a baby anymore but sometimes she *needed* to feel like one. All of us had grown up too fast.

Durme, durme mi alma donzeya
Sleep, sleep my beautiful child

Durme, durme sin ansia i dolor
Sleep without worry or sorrow.

Most days we crowded together on the deck. The sailors passed out biscuits, raisins, a lemon, sometimes dates and bad-smelling olives. There was never enough water. We were always thirsty and many of the girls had dry, swollen tongues.

Unfamiliar illnesses invaded us. Most suffered from what the monks called *queimadura de sol* or burns from the sun. They were like the burns I got when I was careless with Mama's cooking pot. The sores hurt – the skin turned bright red and painful. Sometimes white blisters formed or skin peeled off in little flakes. The worst cases developed fevers and glassy eyes. For the lucky ones like me and Tama, the red healed into an unfamiliar brown skin color. The unlucky ones got thirsty and sick – some even died.

The monks ignored it. They called it the pain of becoming Novos Christaos – we were paying for our parents' sins. That made them work harder. They drilled us in Christian prayers insisting we learn how to properly worship our new lord and savior, Jesus Christ. I already knew some of the prayers but I never let anyone know – the knowledge that I had been raised Converso would make both monks and Jews hate me.

I kept my secrets.

"Pray harder," they railed, "and you will be saved."

Saved? From what Jesus Christ had given us when we were kidnapped from our families? It made no sense but there was no logic in anything.

The worst part of the voyage was the stomach sickness. Some called it *mar doentes* – seasickness. Everyone got it except the sailors. Dizzy, stomach seizing, the world swirled around us. The monks would force us to vomit into the ocean. It we didn't have time and vomited on the deck, we had to clean it up. When the monks and boys got sick, the girls were forced to clean up after them as well.

Tama and I recalled Alvaro de Caminha's words.

You will eat your food and send your sickness overboard.

We didn't want to be eaten by the sea demons or ripped apart, limb by limb, by the degradados. After a week, the sea sickness passed for most of us. A few never got better. Some died after several weeks because they couldn't keep down food or water.

When most of us were able, the monks made us sit on the splintery deck and listen to them beneath an unrelenting sun. They ranted about how Hebrew was the language of Lucifer. It was banned from our minds and tongues forever. I knew they could ban it from my tongue – but not my head. No one could hear what I thought or said *inside.* I was determined to share my few words of Hebrew with Tama once we arrived at São Tome.

They drilled us in prayers and religion and stories of Satan's revenge on people that didn't follow the true path to Jesus Christ. We had to say the same prayer many times during the day.

Sweet Lord Jesus defend me, giving my body strength and my soul health, enduring me with the will to do what is right, and to live justly in this world, and not to fail. Grant me remission of all my sins. Lord, save me waking, save me sleeping, that I may sleep in peace and awake in Thee in the glory of paradise.

We made the sign of the cross before and after the prayer.

Often sailors stood around us and cracked whips over our heads when someone fell asleep. They had evil smiles and hungry eyes like Simao. We were only allowed to speak Portuguese and Latin used in Christian prayer. The monks ignored the sailors unless they had to discipline us. Then they invited the dirtiest one, dressed in smelly, homespun clothes, to threaten us. Tama shivered when they approached and clung to me tightly.

"You'll be okay," I promised.

It was a lie.

When the monks got angry they threatened to "toss us" into the *degradado* section. All eyes turned to the awful, filthy men chained to one another on the other side of the ship. They were starved, got little water and smelled like foul animals squeezed into a tiny barn. Every day the sailors went through the degradados section with heavy axes to chop apart the chains of the dead. They pulled out the bodies, wrapped each corpse in coarse cloth and rolled them overboard as a monk recited a sharp, bitter prayer:

I commend your soul to the loving arms of our Merciful Savior, Jesus Christ.

I wondered how Jesus Christ . . . or any God, could love those pitiful creatures?

5

There was no warning. The wind shifted and it felt like we were in the middle of magic. The sun was high in the sky, the air cooled by a sea breeze, and the clouds drifted like puffs of sheep's wool. Tama pointed to the water and I screamed.

Peixes gigantes.

Giant fish! They were beautiful, silver creatures with silky-smooth skin that swam around the ship. They weren't the sea demons that Alvaro de Caminha described. Instead, the creatures danced and played gracefully as if in the middle of their own game. One leaped into the air and I saw the creature smile. How could I be afraid of a smiling fish?

"Peixes gigantes," I yelled, laughing.

One of the older boys, standing against the rail, laughed with me, his pale brown eyes sparkling in the sun.

"No," the boy shook his head and smiled crookedly. "It's called a *golfinho.*" He lowered his voice. "In Spanish it's a *delfín.*" Dolphin.

Our eyes met.

"Delfín," I echoed him.

He nodded and I smiled. We stared at each other for a very long time.

"My name is Elias," he reached his hand across the barrier between the boys and girls section. Our fingers touched.

"Elias," I said softly. "My name is Esperanza."

"I know. I watch you with the little one."

"Tama?"

"Yes."

I didn't know what to say. "Delfín – I like that name." Then my breath did strange things.

"Do you like the delfin?" I gasped.

"They're magical. They tell us . . . ," he lowered his voice, "Hashem's world can be beautiful. That we're Jews, not chattel belonging to monks and Jesus Christ."

"Don't speak like that – the monks will punish you."

"I don't care. They can't take my soul. That belongs to the God of Moses."

"They can take your life."

"So?"

"Are you sure? Would the God of Moses allow children to be stolen from their mamas and papas?"

"We're the chosen. We suffer the best . . . and the worst . . . that men have to offer. If you believe that, we'll survive."

Our eyes spoke to one another.

I was only a child. Elias was only a child. Yet something connected – a link in a chain that refused to be broken.

Tama grabbed my arm and pointed. "Delfín," she said sweetly.

"Delfín." I smiled.

"Delfín," Elias laughed.

Tama giggled and her dark eyes sparkled. We looked at each other with special understanding. Sisters. Like Hanna. You don't have to share blood to be a sister.

Laughing, Tama counted the creatures. One, two, three Delfin. Then four, five, and six. She could hardly keep track of them.

I will never forget the beautiful, silvery delfín and its grin when it leaped from the sea. Or Elias' words convincing me that we would survive. I'll always remember the odd feeling that suddenly returned – perhaps there really was some hope left for us. All in the middle of an endless ocean, surrounded by *degradados,* hungry sailors, monks and their curses against Jews . . . so many ugly things.

And Elias' touch.

6

Days passed with more sightings of delfin. Elias and I began to meet, our fingertips touching. We talked and laughed and searched the sea. Tama watched, her eyes wide with curiosity. She didn't say anything. I wondered if she knew what was happening. How could she? I didn't know what was happening.

Elias and I shared secrets in the ocean breeze and fiery sun. At night, beneath the stars, we revealed stories of our families and our grief.

One moonless night, Elias took my hand. "Now I will tell you my secret."

I looked into his eyes and knew that it was a gift.

"I'm a kinsman of Don Isaac ben Yehuda Abravanel," he confided.

I gasped. Isaac Abravanel was a hero to the Jews. He was hated by his persecutors. If the monks knew that Elias was related to Abravanel . . .

"He was a great man. Above all, he loved the God of Moses."

Elias stared out at the dark sea. "He had a lot of money and people hated him for that. Everyone knew that he was a "tax farmer" – collecting royal revenues for King Ferdinand. Even worse, he loaned 1,500,000 *maravedi*s to help Ferdinand and Isabella win the war in Grenada."

I knew Abravanel was a Jewish scholar and philosopher who was friend and collaborator with royalty. I shuddered.

"What most people don't know," Elias continued, "was that he offered 30,000 ducats to get King Ferdinand and Queen Isabella to rescind the Edict of Expulsion. They refused. Instead, they demanded that he be baptized. Abravanel was horrified. He returned home, smuggled his son into Portugal and left the country with the other Jews, headed for Naples."

"You must be very proud."

"There's something else. I am an Abravanel kin . . . but I come from a different land."

"I don't understand."

"They call us *Ashkenazi* because we come from the north – on the continent."

"Where?"

"We started out in Germany and then moved north. Some of our customs are different and instead of speaking Ladino we use Yiddish."

"I don't understand."

"You don't have to. You just need to know that sometimes I'm different . . ."

"What were you doing in Spain?"

"Visiting. Learning. Studying differences in our customs. Don Isaac encouraged me. He didn't want separations among Jews. He loved his people."

"Does it matter? That you're Ashkenazi and I'm Sephardic?"

"No – but some people don't like Ashkenazi. They say we're peasants . . ."

I laughed. "How can the kinsman of Abravanel be a peasant?"

"It sounds crazy but people aren't always open-minded."

"Like Ferdinand and Isabella?"

"Yes – and King Joao."

"They hate the Jews."

"Yes."

"Why?"

Elias shrugged. "Maybe it's because we're God's Chosen People – we get the best and the worst of everything."

I tried to understand Elias's story. Abravanel had everything – money, connections, and respect in court. He chose to remain a Jew and leave Spain with his people. On top of it all, Elias wasn't a native – he came from a place where they called themselves Ashkenazi.

I made a decision. If Elias was willing to share his secret, I would share mine.

"I have to tell you something," I whispered to Elias. "It might make you hate *me*."

Elias was very quiet.

"I was born . . . a Converso."

Many Jews hated Conversos because they kept their faith secret and *pretended* to be Christian. People felt that unlike Abravanel, we had made the coward's choice. Briefly I thought of my ancestors who lost two sons to the soldier's swords. Die or save their children? I knew they had made the right choice and I would have done exactly the same thing as them.

Elias froze. He said nothing for a very long time. Then he picked up my hand and gently kissed my fingertips.

I held my breath.

Elias lifted his head. "Like my kinsmen, we crossed the border. There were many of us – my parents, siblings, and cousins. Abravanel gave us money to pay the border tax and find a home on the hill that led up to Castelo de Sao Jorge. My family believed we were safe in Portugal. They trusted King Joao II. Until the day papa and his brothers took the children to the countryside. Mama didn't feel well, so I stayed with her. That was the day the soldiers came."

"Your family is still alive?"

"They were when I left. Who knows by now? Word is that the King wants to break all of us . . . force us to be baptized. With Abravanel blood in us we will never accept."

"No."

"I don't care that you were a Converso – if you don't care that I'm Ashkenazi. We're both different. That means we belong together."

Belong together?

"Mama is still alive," Tama said sleepily. We didn't know if she had heard Elias. "Yes she is," I lied, thinking of the Simao running his sword straight through her heart.

Tama smiled. Elias and I looked at one another and leaned closer. Suddenly a monk shouted over our heads.

"A boy and a girl. Touching. He's a sinful Judaizer. Seize him."

I screamed as the monks pushed me away and grabbed Elias.

"Nooooooo."

They didn't listen. One monk beat him – while another held Elias' arms. The monk's fist landed squarely on his nose, sending blood dripping down his chin.

"Punish him," the monk cried like he was chanting to Jesus Christ. "In the name of our Lord and Savior Jesus Christ, punish the sinner."

"Punish him," another monk joined the litany.

I clawed at the monk's robe. "No . . . we were just talking . . ."

The monk kicked me and I fell, sprawled across the deck. I didn't feel pain, just fear for Elias. Tama, now wide awake, bent over me.

"He'll be ok, Esperanza. I know he'll be ok."

How could she know that? How could anyone know that? I struggled to my feet but it was too late. The monks tossed Elias among the degradados. Everyone turned away. No one wanted to see Elias raped, beaten, or torn apart. I watched with horror as the chained men surrounded Elias. I prayed, with every bit of strength, that our God would protect him.

I couldn't see Elias anymore. I waited throughout the night for a glimpse of him between the chained bodies. Nothing. The evil degradados were too clever. Tama comforted me as I trembled with anger and fear.

"I don't want to lose him," I whispered to her.

"They're eating him for dinner," a monk said, overhearing me. "It serves you right for letting the swine touch you."

"He didn't touch me," I cried.

The monk snorted. "Sinner."

"Puta," the sailors called. "Puta, puta, puta."

I covered my ears, trying to block the horrible word that had condemned Hanna.

"God will protect him," Tama tried to keep me strong.

It didn't help. Over the next few days I could hear Elias's screams and the degradados rattle their chains as if in a deadly game. I couldn't eat or drink. Tama tried to force me but nothing went down. It was a new sickness that I didn't understand. How could the kinsman of Don Isaac Abravanel meet such an ugly fate? Tears clouded my eyes as I waited and watched. I thought of the corpses of degradados thrown overboard and the dead children, wrapped in coarse cloth rolled into the sea beneath plaintive Latin prayers. I recalled the sailors who had been publically flogged. They were all angry men. Why should Elias be spared? The days with Mama and Papa felt like a world ago. Hanna, lying in the dust was my reality. Hanna and Elias and Tama. Why? Why did they hate us? There were no answers so I waited, praying for Elias until sleep took me.

"Esperanza, wake up. Wake up. He's back."

Tama's voice startled me. I had fallen asleep at the spot where Elias had kissed my fingers.

"Back?"

"Elias. They letting him come back from the degradados."

Suddenly there was a wave of catcalls and curses from the degradados. Some wielded their fists like weapons, others screamed their rage. Elias stumbled from their midst.

We watched as he fell to his knees beneath the eyes of grinning monks.

"So boy," one monk said, "you learned your lesson?"

Elias nodded, barely able to hold up his head.

"Should we let you back?"

"For the grace of God, our Lord and Savior Jesus Christ, please. Please let me return to you . . . the fold . . . loyal Christians."

"You will never seduce a woman child again?"

"Never. My love is for Christ."

The monks looked at one another, smiling. "Now you are Christian."

Elias picked up his head. "Bless you. You have taught me the way."

He glanced at me and in that moment I knew Elias was lying.

7

It was several days until Elias told me what happened with the degradados. He whispered in the night shadow, afraid the moonlight might reveal him.

"They were just . . . men," Elias explained. "Men dragged to the dungeons because of debt or theft or other small crimes. Exiled, like the Jews. Just men, Esperanza. They didn't hurt me. I taught them how to ease the pain from their chains with cool water that splashed up from the ocean. I showed them how to catch the rainwater in their hands and drink because it was fresh and it would help them make it to São Tomé. We talked and shared stories about our families and loved ones. Every so often they had me scream as if in pain. They made sure no one could see and laughed at my performance. 'That will make the monks very happy' they said and jangled their chains to make a lot of noise.

They never hurt me. They told me to be more careful when you and I spoke. There would be time and opportunity once we reached the island. The monks were restless, angry because they had been sent to São Tomé. They were always looking to beat anyone . . ."

"They didn't hurt you?"

Elias smiled. "No."

"Then why did you say the words when you were let out? Why did you beg the monks to take you back?"

Elias smiled crookedly. "That's what the degradados told me. They gave me the words and said I didn't have to *feel* them. Say the words and think something different in my head."

I laughed. "You would have made a good Converso."

"Yes, I would have. Now when we reach the island we'll be together," he promised. "With Tama."

I wanted to believe him. I just didn't know how that could ever happen. Yet strange feelings assaulted me – feelings I never experienced before.

"Is that love?" I asked Tama.

She had no answer. She was too young to know.

São Tomé

1

I heard the call.

The sun was deadly hot, hanging in the cloudless sky like a soldier's weapon. Everyone was listless from the heat.

São Tomé ahead.

The sailor dangled from the crow's nest and yelled it again, his voice rough and excited, drunk with discovery.

Monks, children and sailors rushed to the ship's rails, eager to catch the first glimpse of our new home.

"We're here," Tama said softly.

I met Elias's eyes across the deck. Although we couldn't touch, we spoke with our eyes. Whenever he got the chance, Elias sneaked close to us and passed extra bits of biscuits and raisins so we had more to eat. I refused but he always insisted.

"I'm stronger than you and Tama. I can do without but you need the food."

He was right. Tama and I were getting weaker. Some of the children got so weak that they died. Others just lay in the hold, sick and exhausted.

"I can't let you get sick," Elias whispered.

In a strange twist, the degradados had ignited Elias's Abravanel blood. He *was* stronger.

The sailor from the crow's nest bellowed again.

São Tomé ahead.

It had been two long months at sea as Alvaro de Caminha promised. I saw him often during that time. He paced the ship, stared hard at his officers and eagerly declared punishments to the sailors. He attended the floggings, a grim smile pasted on his lips. Was he cruel or was he like Elias, acting for everyone? I would never know the answer. Tama and I stayed far away from him, making sure to carry out his advice.

You will listen to everything the monks tell you.

You will eat your food, send your sickness overboard, and stay quiet and out of way. Perhaps then you will be kept from the sea demons and the degradados *who eat little girls like you for dinner.*

I followed every rule . . . except for Elias. We didn't touch again but we talked secretly in the shadows when no one but Tama could hear.

"Look," Elias pointed excitedly, our eyes meeting briefly.

I followed his hand as the sailor in the crow's nest called out again.

São Tomé ahead.

In the distance, São Tomé looked beautiful – an exotic island with pale brown beaches and strange plants they call *palmeiras*, palm trees. As we drew closer to shore the sun got hotter, the ocean winds died and birds squawked overhead heralding our arrival. We watched the lone island mountain rise like a stone church, surrounded by jungle so dense I wondered how people or animals could live there.

Elias was suddenly at my side. "It looks beautiful," he whispered, "but the degradados say it's very dangerous."

"Dangerous?"

"A terrible fever lives here – one that kills many people.

"I don't understand."

Elias shook his head. "That's why Alvaro de Caminha was sent here. The Donatario da Ilha de São Tomé before him was Joao de

Pereira. He lasted only three years. Before him was Joao de Paiva. He lasted five years. They both died from the fever."

I was stunned.

"Most of us will die."

"Not us."

"No, not us."

Elias's eyes narrowed. His skin was so dark from the sun he looked more like a Moor than a Jew.

"God will protect us," he added unconvincingly.

I nodded. I really wanted to scream the words.

God didn't protect us before. He let the Christians steal us from our homes and families; he let them put us on this boat and watched when so many died, their bodies rolled over into the sea teaming with hungry monsters.

Elias's eyes burned and I knew not to say the words. I was a Converso; he was an Abravanel.

The Sao Gabriel slowed as it crept closer to shore. When the sails caught the last gust of wind from the ocean, Caminha ordered the sailors to lower the anchor and unfurl the sails.

We had arrived.

The *Sao Gabriel* was anchored in a small cove shared with other carracks that had left Lisboa with cargoes of Jewish children and degradados. As we bobbed in the water, I looked at the other ships. It was like a mirror: dark, burned faces stared back – thin, starved bodies hung over the rails, hands grasping the wood. They had a haunted look in their eyes that I knew reflected my own.

Elias tried to reassure us. "We'll be safe, you, me, and Tama. We'll stick together."

Tama clung to my arm and I nodded. I believed Elias.

The sailors lowered the first small rowboat to go ashore with Alvaro de Caminha. They had a ritual when a new carrack arrived – the captain went directly to a large wood cross thrust in the sand.

A small rickety wooden dock stretched over the sand and near the cross. Dozens of people waited for the rowboat. Many had skin darker than Moors, the color of black olives. Others were white. The people stood and waved at the rowboat. The black men were barefoot and wore strange, rag-like skirts tied around their waists. The white men were half-naked and wore woven palm hats for shade. Their skin was red from the sun, bodies damp from the steamy heat, and their chests heaved struggling to breathe. Monks, dressed in traditional robes constantly wiped the sweat off their faces.

The only buildings were pitiful hovels, shabbier than Aldonca and Goncallo's hovel. A dirt trail led from the beach into the jungle beyond. Between the leaves I saw a few larger buildings the color of wet sand.

My throat thickened and it was hard to breathe. São Tomé looked like a nightmare.

The girls, boys, monks, and degradados were strangely quiet. Not knowing what else to do, the monks led a quick prayer onboard. No one paid attention. We wondered when it would be our time to go ashore.

"After Caminha is finished," Elias whispered, "they'll row us to the island."

I watched as Caminha leaped out of the small boat, followed by his officers, into knee-deep water. They waded ashore. No one cared about getting wet. It was too hot.

Caminha was greeted by a group of white men and monks. The black men held back, watching the exchange. I couldn't hear what they said but they seemed very formal. The small group crossed the sand and knelt in front of the cross.

"Pray," one of the monks cried on board. "Pray with our captain to our Lord and Savior Jesus Christ." The monks chanted a hymn as Caminha and his group on land lowered their heads in front of the cross.

Stay with us, Lord, and with Thy light
illume the soul's abyss;
scatter the darkness of our night
and fill the world with bliss.

Elias wrinkled his nose. "As if Christ did us a favor."

"Shhhhh, the monks will beat you."

"They already have and I'm still a Jew and an Abravanel."

2

Alvaro de Caminha had decided, before we arrived, exactly who was allowed to join his colony. Only the strong and healthy could go ashore. The sick and weak had a few weeks to regain their health. If they didn't get better, they would stay on the Sao Gabriel. Caminha didn't want any more sickness on the island. When the ship sailed, the sick and weak would be aboard for a short time. As soon as the carrack reached deep water they would be tossed to the sea demons, dead or alive. No one but sailors returned to Lisboa.

Many children had already died. I feared for the sisters who were thin and weak, shivering with fever every night. I wondered about the little boy who had been ill with mar doentes for the entire voyage, his face deathly pale from the sea sickness. I questioned what would happen to the three older girls used each night by the sailors and returned, broken by their ordeal. It was said that one of them was pregnant. If the sailors knew they would throw her overboard. The three of us were tired but healthy while Elias's friend, flogged by a sailor for stealing food, had festering wounds that refused to heal. Would he become food for the sea demons?

Half of the degradados, chained and constantly exposed to the sun, rain, and wind, had already died. They also watched the shore waiting for Caminha's ritual to be completed.

No one aboard the Sao Gabriel knew their fate.

Finally Caminha rose from the sand followed by monks and white men. He turned to the Sao Gabriel and waved. It was time to come ashore.

The boys went first. Some were afraid of jumping into the rowboats so they were tossed overboard to the sailors. They screamed as the sailors caught them and dropped them hard into the small boats that bobbed with the impact. Many of the boys screamed. The sailors laughed and spat into the water. The girls watched, knowing it would soon be our turn. Tama and I clung to one another as I wondered if we had lost Elias.

Elias waved from his boat and mouthed the words.

I'll find you.

We waved back as the sailors rowed to shore.

It felt like hours before the last rowboat filled with children left the Sao Gabriel. After us, the degradados would be unchained and rowed ashore. I wondered how many would make the trip. The assassinos e ladroes didn't scare me since Elias's experience with them.

I prayed they would be safe.

3

São Tomé looked like an enchanted creature rising from the water. Thick jungles lay beyond the beach – a mountain hovered like royalty above them. I squeezed Tama's hand and she smiled bravely as we jumped into the rowboat that would take us ashore. The waves were rough, jolting the tiny boat loaded with children. The sailors rowed hard to stay on course. When we approached the beach black men waded into the water to drag our boat ashore.

Like Caminha, we waded through shallow water to the brown sand beach. The water felt cool in the suffocating heat. I held Tama's hand tightly. We stood for a moment on the sand giggling over the feel of solid land.

Maybe São Tomé wasn't that bad? I stared up at the sun. It was so hot! Hotter than I ever experienced. The air was thick and damp like steam rising from a cooking pot. The black-olive-colored people on shore seemed comfortable. They were lean with big eyes and bright smiles. The white men were red and angry. Many were puffy and fat, dripping rivers of sweat that made them smell like barn animals. The monks, red-faced in their heavy robes, prepared to herd us but we were children and it had been a long voyage. Land felt so good. Impulsively, the children scattered, breaking apart the well-ordered groups of boys and girls. Suddenly Elias was with us. Without thinking, we hugged – Tama first and then me. I backed away shyly. Something stirred inside but I didn't have much time to think about it. Monks and sailors were shouting, cursing, and threatening the children, desperately trying to keep us together.

No one listened.

Without thinking, I hugged Elias again. "I'm so glad . . ."

A strange light filled his dark eyes. He smiled crookedly.

Tama watched, her head tilted, not sure of what she saw.

Without warning, we heard a joyous scream. We broke apart to see children racing to a golden-colored beach scattered with big black rocks. Everyone was yelling – it was impossible to distinguish the words from the wind and the happy calls of the kids. There was a joy – a sense of freedom – that the adults couldn't contain. The monks tried to grab arms, the fat white men jumped in their path, and the agile black men raced after them.

"Let's go," I laughed.

Elias held us back. "No, there's something wrong."

"What can be wrong with a beach?"

"Look. The black men are trying to stop them."

"They don't want us to have fun."

Tama started to cry. "Let's go!"

"It's more than that. It feels like . . ."

His voice was eaten by the wind as the fastest-running children reached the beach – two boys from another carrack. They ran so hard that they never saw what was coming.

"The rocks are moving," Elias shouted, panic in his voice.

He was right. We saw what the children missed. The children stopped running; the sailors and monks didn't have to hold anyone back. The white men paused, unwilling to move forward. The black men stopped and watched helplessly, their eyes downcast.

The rocks were alive. They transformed into horrible, scaly monsters with mouths the size of wood carts and sharp evil teeth in long, wavy jaws. Sea demons on the beach? The boys were racing each other and never saw what was coming. They leaped on the sand and the black rocks surrounded them.

"Crocodiles," Elias whispered thickly. "I heard about them from the degradados."

Suddenly one of the boys turned and met my eyes. I knew immediately who it was – my friend Palos. The boy who played with me and Isabel – who knew me in the tunnels as a Secret Jew and in the town as another child, best friends with Catholic Isabel. The three of us were always together, laughing playing . . .

What was Palos doing in São Tomé?

I recalled Rosada's laugh in the warehouse in Lisboa.

It's an island where giant lizards eat children!
We're all going to die – the lizards will have us for dinner.

I saw children beaten and Black Death victims die, their faces covered with pustules. I saw live men tossed in the sea, pulled underwater and eaten by monsters who left trails of blood bubbles on the surface. I saw sailors and *degradados* flogged, their screams filling the air as the Sao Gabriel rocked jauntily in the ocean. None of it prepared me to see Palos torn apart by crocodiles on a golden beach beneath a cheerful blazing sun.

There was no rescue. The other children turned as if one body and raced *away* from the beach. Monks grabbed the littlest ones to help them move faster. The men pushed and pulled the older children. The air was filled with screams, pocked by the squawks of seabirds gathering overhead for offal and the oddly soothing slap of waves against the sand.

I froze, ignoring Tama's and Elias' cries to drag me further away.

Caminha appeared. He watched, not moving. A harsh smile played on his lips.

"They will learn now," he snarled.

4

I covered Tama's eyes but it was too late.

Palos smiled sadly and mouthed the word, *adios.* Then the crocodiles lunged. They tore off arms and legs, sending blood in all directions. Palo's head, along with the other boy, was tossed like a ball of wool. In minutes, they were bloody heaps of flesh that the monsters fought one another for the best tidbits.

My throat was thick – my stomach did a nauseating dance like the mar doentes on the ship.

"You knew him?" Elias asked gently.

I nodded. Palos and Isabel. My best friends.

The children ran away from the beach and the crocodiles. Some were crying. Others silent. Everyone was stunned by the massacre.

They waited silently with the black men, white men, monks, sailors, degradados, and Alvaro de Caminha.

"This is an evil place," Elias whispered.

"São Tomé is not a holiday," Alvaro de Caminha snarled with the look of the crocodiles in his eyes. "It's a place to work. Welcome to your new home." He turned and strode away, disappearing between the palms.

I hated him – almost as much as I hated São Tomé.

The monks led us from the beach. No one spoke. No one fought them. The children fell into lines as we filed down the lone path. The palms grew thicker; plants, flowers, and bushes choked the path, forcing us to pick our way through branches, leaves, and roots. Elias stayed behind us, not touching. I could *feel* him there like a sentry. I wasn't sure who we needed protection against – the adults or the monsters.

Both, Mama warned in my head.

I touched my hamsa. It was warm. From the sun or air or something else?

I'm so sorry, Palos. Another piece of my past had been wrenched away before my eyes. What was next? I would never say his name again.

After a few minutes we reached a small compound pressed up against the jungle. It was divided into two sections and surrounded by a low fence.

"The gate is never closed," Elias said softly.

The girls and youngest children lived on one side, separated by a low barrier from the boys. The "house" was a flimsy structure with a palm-leaf room and partially open walls. It was filled with beds made from leaves. Each bed had a tiny pile of personal belongings.

No one worried about escape from the compound because there was no where to go. The jungle was thick and impenetrable. Who wanted to go back to the beach? We were trapped.

"Meet me at the fence," Elias whispered as he went to the boy's side.

Tama and I looked inside the girl's compound. The shelter had been built quickly and sloppily. The monks told us to find a pile of leaves and call it our beds. Tama and I found two "beds" in the corner closest to the outside yard and boy's compound. We put a few rocks in the middle to show it was our spot.

The air was hot and humid – insects buzzed constantly. It was hard to breathe, like swallowing air through a bucket of water. The children from all of the boats were shoved together. We met girls that weren't on the Sao Gabriel but had similar experiences on their voyage. Many of their companions had died during the voyage. Brothers, sisters, and cousins searched for one another. There wasn't a family that hadn't lost someone.

The children mourned them along with their parents. When the monks weren't looking, the older children said Hebrew prayers that they had committed to memory. Some of us sat close, not remembering the words but recognizing the melodies and moving our lips along with those who did. They said kadish for their loved ones who died.

Yit'gadal v'yit'kadash sh'mei raba
We listened and warned them if the monks were coming.

A few younger children still cried from homesickness while the older ones, like me, tried to comfort them.

Gradually, we settled into our new lives.

The monks came to drill us about Jesus Christ. They were slow-moving and exhausted in their heavy robes. The sweat dripped down their bodies until they smelled like the stacks of garbage next to the food tent. We never said anything about their body odor . . . we were afraid of a beating or being thrown to the crocodiles. The monks were hot and cranky – they loved to threaten us with the crocodiles or whack us with bamboo if we didn't behave, were caught whispering, or holding our noses when they passed. They gave us food, mostly fruit from the jungle, bits of stale bread, and never enough water.

Everyone was deadly hot. It wasn't long before we learned about the *enfermaria* – the sick tent where people went to die from the fever.

5

Elias came to visit each night, hiding beneath the leaves of a giant, sprawling plant. We talked, we cried and we laughed. We never knew what would happen next. One night, before they started the work details, Elias hid with us beneath the bush. We talked about our families, our old lives, and the good things left behind.

"I miss them so much. Mama and Papa and Hanna. I fear for their lives."

Elias nodded. "We will never know."

"Maybe it's better."

"Maybe."

I sighed. Very quietly, Tama began to cry. I cradled her in my arms and spoke softly, singing Mama's lullaby. Elias watched, his shoulder pressed up against mine. His eyes filled with a strange light.

Durme, durme mi alma donzeya
Sleep, sleep my beautiful child

Finally, Tama fell asleep. I laid her across a soft bed of leaves.

Elias shuddered. "We all lost so much."

"I wonder if Tama will remember her mama when she grows up."

Elias pressed closer to me. I should have been scared. I should have moved away but it felt good.

"We have each other," he said thickly.

"Yes."

Without warning, Elias leaned over and kissed me. I had never been kissed before. At first I wanted to run away from him. It was so wrong. Young girls didn't kiss boys until they married. Then a voice in my head shifted. This was São Tomé – the old rules no longer worked.

Elias pulled away. "I'm sorry. I shouldn't have done that."

"I liked it."

Then I did something I would have never even thought about in my old life. I pulled his face to mine and kissed him again.

It was as if we were transported to a different place and time. Something warm and delicious stirred inside. Hope seeped back into my soul. Elias trembled and kissed me harder, his breath suddenly ragged. Was I hurting him?

Tama stirred in her sleep and we pulled apart.

"I . . ."

I smiled and stroked his cheek, feeling sprouts of hair that would eventually grow into a beard.

"We're not children anymore."

"No, we're not children. We've been through too much."

"So it's okay?"

"It's okay."

We kissed again.

"I think . . . I think I might love you."

I giggled.

We kissed . . . again and again until the compound disappeared, the jungle faded, and the heat came from inside rather than the thick air that surrounded us.

Reluctantly, Elias pulled away. "I have to leave before they notice I'm gone."

I nodded as he stood up, towering over me and Tama. He left slowly, slinking out from the protection of the plant, beneath more bushes, and back into the boy's compound. I didn't want to move, didn't want to think of anything but Elias's kisses. I curled up next to Tama and thought about his words.

I think . . . I think I might love you.

Did I love Elias? Was this what it felt like? I thought about the heat *inside* me and how the ugly compound disappeared and the jungle faded when he kissed me.

No, Esperanza, we're not children. We've been through too much.

If we weren't children anymore did that mean we could love like adults? I fell asleep dreaming of Elias.

6

The work details began.

The oldest and strongest boys were assigned to the sugar cane fields. They followed a path through the dense jungle. Elias was one of them. I feared for his safety – if Tama was right about monsters in the jungle, what would happen to him?

The older girls were split up. Some gathered fruit and food for the livestock. Tama and I joined them. Others were assigned to clean the compound, help with the cooking or work with the sick in the enfermaria.

We were on São Tomé for a few weeks when the fever hit. It ran rampant through the compound, killing victims more effortlessly than crocodiles. The enfermaria was filled when we arrived – two weeks later it was bursting. Many sick children remained in the compound getting worse until they died. Every day someone new got the fever and every day someone died. They were racked with chills although the air was hot. They shook violently even though they burned with fever. They shivered from the cold and their skin was covered with sweat. Many cried out from pains in their heads and bodies. Some coughed; some had foul-smelling, watery stools and vomited. None could stand up from the fatigue that came with the fever. When the end came they convulsed in jerky movements, foam forming on their lips. No one could stop the shaking. Others turned yellow. Some just drifted off into a sleep where they didn't wake up. So many died that there were many piles of leaves – "beds" left empty. Rosada died. Sacca, who carried her little sister in her arms, died. Ysabel, Garti, Payna, Gatel and Myarra all died. And that was only the beginning.

Tama, Elias and I were spared. I don't know why. Maybe God decided to intervene? Elias said that some people got the fever and never knew it; others never got it at all. Most of the white people who were infected would die. The black men never got sick.

Maybe Caminha was right . . . Ilha de São Tomé was a death sentence.

Elias and I continued to meet beneath the shadows of night and our sprawling plant. We talked and played with Tama until her eyes got heavy and she fell asleep. Then we kissed. The kisses got deeper and stronger until it felt like my entire body was focused on my lips. I knew it was wrong but I couldn't stop. Elias couldn't stop. We continued breaking tradition. Sometimes, after kissing until it was hard to breathe, we held one another and talked about what was happening in the compound, the dying children and the rumors. Then we built new dreams.

"We'll get out of here. Abravanels need to be free."

I wondered what he meant. It felt like his words were more about our kisses than the compound.

"Yes. We'll make our own house, find our own food, be with our own God . . ."

Elias grinned and kissed me again.

My body began to change. My breasts grew and my waist narrowed and I hungered more for Elias's kisses. Mama had told me about the blood, so when it happened I wasn't surprised. I told Elias and he celebrated with me.

"You're a woman now," he laughed, kissing me.

I recognized that being a woman in the girl's compound on São Tomé was a dangerous thing.

"Each night," I told Elias, "men come from the huts and take the oldest girls. They use them and defile them. When they're finished, they return the girls to the compound, crying, bleeding, broken, and dishonored."

"They make them into whores," he grimaced.

"No one cares."

"The monks?"

"They say it's a good thing for the men. It makes them stronger for the fields."

"And the girls?"

"Who cares about some Jewish girls? They're murdering them like Hanna . . ."

Elias was very quiet.

"Some of the girls are pregnant."

"They will have the devil's children."

"They won't even know the father of their child."

"The men are devils."

I shook my head. "That makes no difference."

"And you?" Elias took a deep breath. "Have they come for you . . . or Tama?"

"No. Tama is too little and I look younger than my age. But I can't help . . . growing up. It's only a matter of time. No one is spared."

"Cover yourself," Elias growled, "don't let them see how beautiful you are."

I smiled in the shadows. "I think you love me."

Instead of laughing, Elias snarled like a wild dog. "I won't let that happen to you."

I liked his jealousy. "The gate is open," I said seductively, "all we have to do is slip out at night . . ."

"Go where?"

"You go out each day to the fields. What's there?"

Elias scratched his dark curls. "When we go to the sugar cane fields we work hard – long hours, backbreaking work . . ."

"What's past the fields?"

"I don't know. The jungle is so thick, I don't know how anyone can get through it . . . but."

"But what?"

"I've heard," he tilted his head conspiratorially, "that way up on the mountain in the middle of the island, there's a fugitive camp."

"What's a fugitive camp?"

"It's a place where people run to . . . hide . . . to get away from this."

"Who lives there?"

"Escaped slaves and their women . . ."

"Mixed bloods and *degradados*."

"You know about it?"

"I heard stories . . ."

"I don't know how safe . . ."

"If we stay here," my voice was shrill, "one of the men will rape me. Maybe Tama too. It's only a matter of time."

"I don't know. I don't know what we might be getting ourselves into . . . it could be worse than here."

"I don't want a filthy man to take me. I don't want to have a baby."

He lowered his head. His voice was threatening, like a warrior. "I have to protect you and Tama. We can't stay here. Tomorrow night, when everyone is asleep, we'll sneak out of the compound. We'll figure it out."

"Thank you," I touched his hand.

"Gather and hide as much bread as you can."

I kissed him. "Tomorrow."

The next day the rains began.

We had to wait.

Revenge

1

Word spread through the compound. The Sao Gabriel returned from Lisboa with a fresh load of soldiers and degradados. No children. At first many of us were happy. They hadn't kidnapped more Jewish children. I thought about the lucky ones – the children who remained with their mamas and papas. Many of us smiled when the new men came ashore. Our smiles quickly turned to frowns. We worried about new hungers – more men coming to the compound to take girls. Tama and I hid beneath a canopy of leaves protected by the relentless downpour when the new soldiers arrived to view the girls. They looked dirty, hot, and hungry. Lust replaced fatigue as they surveyed the compound. We heard they were the worst of the King's soldiers – banished to our island. Tama and I shivered, afraid they might see us hiding.

And then I saw him.

He was ugly with icy snakelike blue eyes, dirty caramel-colored hair, and rotted teeth. Tama's mouth opened with a silent scream. I couldn't breathe. His small eyes were streaked with red and filled with raw hunger. His white skin was charred and he had new scars on his face. He was a snake searching for prey. Although he no longer wore the Red Cross on his chest I knew immediately who he was.

Simao.

The girls whispered that many of the new soldiers were disgraced and sent to São Tomé as punishment. As the days passed, Simao proved to be the worst. The girls were terrified of him. They learned his patterns and hid when they knew he would arrive. Even then, Simao always found someone.

Simao came to the compound several days a week, swooped up his choice and dragged her into the maze of hovels they called town. Sometimes the girl didn't return for days, other times she didn't return at all. No one cared. The Portuguese said it was part of doing duty on *São Tomé*. Their rights. Each day I saw Simao's work in the eyes of the girls he used – glazed and defeated – and in their bodies that were bruised, broken, and beaten.

Like Hanna.

"Don't let him see you," Elias warned. "The rains won't last much longer and then we can escape."

"I have red hair. I'm hard to miss."

"He hasn't seen you yet?"

"No."

"Hide. Hide until I can get you out of here."

"Everyone hides from him now."

"Hide better. You'll be okay. You *have* to be okay. God will protect you."

I doubted Elias.

One night Simao came to the compound earlier than usual. He knew that the girls hid so he tricked them by showing up before they had a chance to take cover. He had his pick.

He chose Miriam, a thin, slight girl who was rigid beneath his grasp. My heart broke for the delicate girl. She would never survive Simao's cruelty. I watched him carry Miriam off, feeling safe for at least another day. I wasn't careful.

Simao saw me.

2

His voice made my skin crawl.

"Ah, my red-headed puta. We meet again." He grinned with rotted teeth and putrid breath. I shrank back but he grabbed my arm.

"Yes, I remember you. We had your sister. Ah, what a delicious piece."

I saw him in my mind bent over Hanna and thrusting himself inside her, between her legs, over and over, ignoring her screams.

He moved closer, towering over me. Hanging on to Miriam, he bent over and roughly felt my breasts as if selecting an animal for slaughter. "I took your sister because you weren't ready. Now my Jew girl, I see you are."

I froze.

"Leave her alone," Tama screamed, leaping at his leg. He kicked her away, sending her flying across the dirt. "I see your little friend is still with you." Simao snarled. "She's still too young, but you . . ."

Suddenly Miriam squirmed in his arms.

"Tonight my red-headed puta, I'm tired. I can only take one girl. I will sleep well and tomorrow I'll be back for you." He laughed and shook Miriam. "She's not pretty but she'll do. Tomorrow . . ." he patted my cheek, "is your turn. You're pretty and fresh, no doubt a virgin." He roared so loud that his spittle splattered my cheek. "I will have this one for dinner and tomorrow you'll be my breakfast."

He bellowed like a wild animal.

"I'm going to fuck you like you've never been fucked before, my Jewish puta. And when I finish, you know what you're going to say? Thank you. Thank you. Thank you." Simao laughed maniacally.

I trembled as if I was sick from the fever.

"I'm going to fuck you so bad you won't know what happened. And it will be the best thing in your life." Simao turned and dragged Miriam out of the compound, howling at his turn of fortune.

Tama scrambled up from the dirt and ran to me. She was trembling so hard I could barely distinguish my own pounding heart.

Tomorrow.

"Will he make a baby in you?" Tama asked.

For a moment I couldn't answer.

He can make a baby. He can also kill me.

I'm out of time.

Although the rains were still heavy I knew that I had to reach Elias and escape.

"We're leaving," I said to Tama.

Tama stared at me for a long time. Instead of crying, she nodded and located the bread we had hidden. I watched her and wondered how I would tell Elias. I couldn't leave without him but if I couldn't find him, I *had* to leave. Alone.

I rolled the bread into leaves – the way the girls in the compound had taught me. I took Tama's hand and plunged into the torrential rains, wading through the mud that led to the boy's compound.

We reached the fence and called Elias's name. No one heard us – or cared – in the driving rain. Tama and I looked at one another. We both knew that we might have to leave without him. A small boy appeared out of nowhere. He wasn't much older than Tama.

"He's sleeping," the boy said grumpily.

"What's your name?"

Straight, blonde hair and heavy eyes showed his suspicion. "Why do you want to know?"

"Elias will be happy you woke him. He'll reward you."

The little boy looked interested. "My name is Roffe."

"I'm Esperanza. This is Tama. Now find Elias and wake him up. Tell him we're here."

Roffe shrugged.

"Please – and hurry."

"Why should I believe you?"

"We're Jews, just like you."

His eyes softened.

"Please – I'm in trouble. The bad man is coming for me tomorrow. He told me. He's going to take me like he took my sister."

Was it the desperation in my voice? Or that Roffe knew – or had seen – a loved one raped? He understood.

"I'll find Elias for you," Roffe said in a voice far beyond his years.

He turned and disappeared in the rain. Tama and I waited, praying Roffe would succeed.

"What if he can't find Elias? Or doesn't want to?"

I couldn't answer Tama's question. I didn't want to frighten her but I knew we had to leave immediately. If Roffe didn't find Elias we were on our own. Maybe dinner for the jungle monsters? I would rather have been food for crocodiles than Simao's dessert. What about Tama? I touched her arm.

"You don't have to come, Tama. You can still go back to the compound and no one will ever know."

Tama shook her head. "Sisters," she said stubbornly.

There was no leaving her behind.

I don't know how long we waited but the rain stopped and a full moon broke through the clouds. Dim light filled the compound and we shrank against the divider. Tama and I were so tired but I fought sleep, kneeling next to her on the ground.

Please Elias. Hear us.

3

"Esperanza! Esperanza!"

My eyes snapped open. It was Elias. I stood up quickly and saw that the sky was beginning to lighten.

"Elias. I'm here."

He reached across the divider and grabbed my hand. "I've been looking for you. Roffe said . . ."

I cut him off. "I think I fell asleep. Tama, too. Elias, we have to get out of here *now*. Simao saw me."

Elias paled.

"He took Miriam and he promised to come back for me tomorrow."

Elias grabbed my hand. "I'll kill him before he touches you."

"How can you kill him, you're just a boy."

"I won't let him take you."

"He can kill you and . . ."

Elias's hands tightened around mine until he was hurting me.

"I love you and I won't let that monster touch you."

Suddenly Tama stood up. She heard everything but didn't respond.

"Let me think. We need a plan." He paused. "We'll leave now before the sun is up. We'll go into the jungle and hide until nightfall and then walk inland to the mountain until we find the fugitive camp."

"I'm so tired," Tama said sleepily.

I put my arms around her. "We have to go."

"I'm going, too."

We followed the voice.

It was Roffe.

"I'm going, too," he repeated stubbornly.

"You can't," Elias said gently. "We're going far, traveling much, and I don't know if there will be food. We might find wild animals . . ."

Roffe' eyes gray eyes widened. "I don't care. I want to be with you."

Elias and I looked at one another.

"Are you sure Roffe? We don't know what's going to happen . . . what's ahead of us."

"It can't be worse than here."

"Yes it can."

"I don't care. I hate it here."

"It doesn't matter. We're not taking you."

"Then I'll wake the monks and tell them. They'll catch you and . . ." he looked at me, "do things."

"You can't threaten us."

"Yes I can. I can make you take me with you." He paused. "Please don't leave me here."

Elias and I exchanged looks. "Okay," Elias decided. "But you have to do everything I tell you."

Roffe nodded.

"No questions, no messing around. You can't cry if you get scared or you want to come back."

"I never want to come back. I hate them."

We all hated them.

"Let's go," Elias said. "They leave the gate open because they know that no one will try to escape – there's no place to go. The guards are probably drunk and sleeping. If we're really quiet we can sneak past them to the trail."

I put my hand out. Elias covered it with his followed by Tama and Roffe.

Four Jewish children. We were in this together.

Elias said some words in Hebrew. "Let's say it together."

Shema Yisrael Adonai Elohaenu Adonai Echad

We left.

4

The rain was lighter and didn't obstruct our vision in the approaching dawn. Dark gray clouds spotted the sky. Elias and Roffe were on one side of the divider and Tama and I on the other. Silently, we made our way to the gate, careful not to splash mud or water, slip on sleeping bodies or disturb trash that lay scattered throughout the compound. It was my only chance to avoid Hanna's fate. If I failed my life would end like my sister's.

Please Mama and Papa and Hanna. Watch over me.

I took a deep breath and looked straight ahead, fighting the fear that claimed my soul. In a short time we saw the gate in front of us. Dangerously close. Our feet were sucked into the mud – they made tiny squishing sounds like grunts. My heart pounded so loudly it felt like it would break. Although I was saturated by the rain, sweat poured down my face, back, and between my breasts.

Tama held my hand so tightly it hurt. She was so small yet so brave. Even Roffe was trembling. Only Elias stood straight and determined.

It was hard to stop from conjuring horrible pictures in my mind. Mama. Papa. Hanna. The people in Lisboa. Simao. The men using girls from the compound. I narrowed my eyes and forced my attention on the gate. I had to be completely alert.

We paused at the gate. There were two guards, both sprawled on the ground, heads turned to the side, snoring loudly. Next to them were empty wineskins once filled with the cheap, brownish stuff they made on the island. The guards were drunk, sleeping it off.

One of them was Simao.

I glanced at Elias. There was nothing to say. The light was coming quickly now and we had to make our move. Beyond the gate was the dirt trail that led into the jungle. It reminded me of another trail just beyond the tunnel with Hanna holding a small lamp as we fled the Inquisitors. Were Simao, the monks, the soldiers, and Alvaro de Caminha any different? Would our fate be any different?

The rains had made the jungle so dense that the new trail was narrow and overgrown. If we made it past the guards we would have to move quickly while picking our way through the undergrowth. The next move was to disappear into the jungle and hide. We couldn't let the morning sugar cane crews see us as they marched to the field. Maybe they wouldn't know we were gone? Perhaps they would assume that Elias had caught the fever? With luck, no one would know we were missing until Simao came for me at the end of the day.

Elias touched my hand. He knew what I was thinking.

Simao stirred and I held my breath. He flipped over, revealing a pool of vomit that he slept in all night. Elias wrinkled his nose in disgust. I thought of everything that happened since the awful night when The Inquisitors knocked at our door. I thought of Mama and Papa, their eyes burning with purpose, their hands shaking as we escaped through the trap door. I remembered the sound of the table dragged over our heads and Hanna's push to move on through the darkness. I thought of Aldonca and Goncallo's hovel and the only peace I felt since leaving home. I saw Tama and her mother reaching for one another on the dock in Lisboa. I looked at the little girl who I vowed to protect. Is that how Mama felt? Is that how Hanna felt? Is that what Elias feels right now?

Simao's snores sounded like a pig grunting. His lips bubbled with each breath, spit trickled down his chin. I shuddered.

"Now, Esperanza. Now!"

Elias nudged me forward and I grabbed Tama's arm. I took a deep breath. I scurried through the mud to the gate. The rain stung my face and the mud sucked at my feet. We slithered between Simao and the other soldier like jungle snakes. One soldier didn't stir. I slowed down and picked my way around Simao. We were almost safe. I made Tama go first . . . I would protect her if anything happened to me.

Suddenly fingers curled around my ankle. Simao was awake! His bloodshot eyes pierced me, his rotted teeth made a jeering smile. He hung onto my ankle. I didn't scream – I didn't want to wake the other guard and risk Tama's life. Simao laughed crazily as he wrenched me down into the mud.

I was trapped.

I struggled to pull my ankle free but Simao held me back.

"Run," I cried to Tama.

Tama stood still.

"My Jewish puta," Simao hissed, "you're not going anywhere." He dragged me closer as I fought wildly. He put his arms around me and pressed his privates against my back. "See what you do to me," he rubbed his crotch against me. "Like your sister. I will have both of you." Simao laughed wildly as flipped me over and pinned me flat in the mud, tucking my arms beneath my body. I twisted and squirmed but to no avail. I was helpless.

Simao mounted me like a dog.

I could hardly breathe, suffocating beneath his weight. Simao reached down and pulled out his hard, erect privates. I freed one arm and clawed at him, the ground, and his hands but he easily overpowered me.

He enjoyed my fight.

For a moment I stared into his blue eyes. Evil. Pure evil. He laughed in delight.

"I'm going to fuck you like you've never been fucked before. And when I finish, you know what you're going to say, my

Jewish puta? Thank you. Thank you. Thank you." Simao laughed maniacally.

"Noooooo."

"I'm going to fuck you so bad you won't know what happened. And it will be the best thing in your life."

His voice stung like a serpent searching for blood. Suddenly I saw Miriam lying in the mud. She was limp and broken, watching Simao rape me. Simao snarled with pleasure as he ripped my clothes and forced my legs apart.

"I have one for dinner and now . . ." he shook with delight, "I'll have one for breakfast."

5

"Run," I cried again to Tama.

Tama flew into motion. She didn't run but turned on Simao, kicking and punching with all her strength. He laughed louder and pushed her away like a bug.

"I have one for dinner . . ." he said again, pleased with his chant, "and now I'll have one for breakfast. And maybe, little Jew girl, I'll have you for lunch as well."

When was this going to end, Mama?

Out of nowhere, there was a whooshing sound. I saw a blur of motion as Simao began to force himself into me. Simao never saw it coming. It was a log, the width of a man's arm. It smashed his head with a sickening thud. Simao fell back. Elias dropped the log and rolled Simao off me. Then Elias lunged for Simao's throat. I rolled away but Simao held on to my arm. Tama and Roffe kicked and punched his body. Simao's fingers slipped off my arm – I wrenched myself free from his grasp. I scrambled to my feet. Trickles of blood ran from the corner of his mouth and his ears. I watched in horror and joy . . . Elias, Tama, and Roffe were doing this for *me*.

I joined them . . . kicking and hitting him with all my strength.

This is for Mama and Papa.

This is for Aldonca and Goncallo.

This is for Hanna.

Although the four of us were small, the anger and loss inside far exceeded our size. We spent it on this evil snake. Suddenly, out of the brush, a man appeared. We froze. He was a big man, with thick muscles on his shoulders, arms, and chest; skin browned from the sun. He stood for a moment to take in the scene. Simao stirred. The four of us backed off, not knowing what to do next.

The man stared at Elias. A small smile played on his lips. "My friend from the Sao Gabriel."

He was one of the degradados. He pulled out a dagger from a pouch on his waist, flipped it over and offered it to Elias.

Elias nodded without smiling.

"I think you can use this," the degradado said.

We stared at the offering. The dagger hung in the space between us, waiting for a decision.

Elias took a deep breath. "Thank you," he whispered and grasped the weapon. He turned to me. "It's your right," Elias said softly. "Take your revenge." He put the knife in my hands.

I stared at the weapon. Mama. Papa. Hanna. Aldonca. Goncallo. Tama's Mama. Using both hands, I grasped the red handle of the dagger. Elias, Tama, Roffe, and the degradado watched. No one breathed.

Simao's eyes fluttered open. He knew what was about to happen. He smiled.

"Do it puta," Simao hissed. "Show me that you're a real Jewish whore like your sister."

I saw red.

Simao grinned. "You'll never be rid of me, Jew girl."

"This is for Hanna," I hissed. "Palos. Goncallo. Tama's Mama."

I raised the dagger and with all my strength plunged it into Simao's heart.

He twitched a few times as the life seeped from the blue eyes. The caramel-colored hair was matted with blood.

You'll never be rid of me.

All eyes were upon him.

Simao was dead.

I stared at my work.

I killed a man. For revenge.

The degradado nodded his approval. "Get out of here," he said and took the dagger from my hands. He wiped the blood off with leaves. "God be with you."

I never knew the degradado's name.

But I never forgot him.

Elias

1

"Let's go," Elias took charge, "before the other soldier wakes up."

I paused. Who would have believed that not so long ago, tucked comfortably with our families and our God, four children would be capable of assault? Who would have believed that I could become a murderer?

Simao was still next to Miriam, covered in his blood and vomit. His eyes were open, staring at nothing. His arms sunk lifelessly in the mud.

I spoke to the sky, barely visible above the dense green. "Now Hanna, wherever you are, you can be at peace."

I glanced at Miriam who watched with dead eyes. Was there a smile on those cracked and bloody lips? I leaned over her. "Come with us. You'll be safe."

Miriam, whose entire body was swollen and purple – distorted by Simao's beatings – smiled weakly. "Leave me." she said softly. "I'm already dead."

"Please – there's hope. There has to be hope."

"Maybe for you. Maybe for them," she tilted her head toward Elias, Tama, and Roffe, "but not for me." Miriam smiled weakly and turned her head away.

"We have to go!" Elias demanded. "*Now.*"

I stared at Miriam. Was Hanna giving me a message? Would I ever know? I took one last look at Miriam but her eyes were closed.

"Please?"

Miriam didn't respond. Was this right? Would I ever forget the joy of *now* – taking the life of a snake who slaughtered children's souls?

"We have to go!" Elias repeated.

There was nothing more to say or do. If we were caught the soldiers and monks would kill us. I was a murderer and they were my accomplices.

Silently, the four of us joined hands. Tama, Elias, Roffe, and me. We *walked* into the jungle together.

It was dense and scary but we were determined.

And free.

2

The jungle was dark, only a touch of morning light penetrated the thick canopy above us. Birds cried, squawked, and sang in the new day. It *was* a new day – although we had no idea where it might bring us.

We picked our way down the trail overgrown with dense plants, roots, and trees. Streaks of sunlight, like trickles of golden water, broke through the canopy. I felt like any minute the soldiers would appear demanding revenge for the murder of their comrade.

Who would miss Simao? Did anyone ever *love* that man of evil?

"This is the lowland jungle," Elias interrupted my thoughts.

I had to refocus my thoughts away from Simao. It could be deadly not to concentrate on what was around me.

I stopped him Mama. I was very brave Papa. I killed him Hanna. It was right. He will never defile another woman again.

Behind us, the compound, hovels, and buildings of the São Tomé colony were gobbled up by jungle as if they no longer existed.

That was good – if we saw them again the monks and soldiers would execute us – perhaps throw us to the crocodiles. I shivered. There was only one way out.

We marched through a strange world, unlike anything I had ever seen before. Everything was painted in shades of green . . . more greens than I knew existed. Thin, lanky trees reached for the sky, flanked by larger, thick-trunked trees that twisted as they battled for light. Sprawling ferns with huge, lacey leaves in all directions were everywhere, tucked amid exotic greenery. Flowers bloomed in impossible colors and shapes. There was a constant chorus from birds and insects. The long, woven nests of shiny black sunbirds dangled from branches. Tiny black and white thrushes took short flights between the leaves while golden brown grosbeaks soared overhead. A pair of lemon-yellow bellied birds paused to watch us while a brightly-colored quail stared from its high perch. The birds dissolved my fear. Before I entered the jungle, I thought it was dangerous, full of death. I was wrong. It throbbed with life in all colors, shapes, and sounds. Elias pointed out the birds and whispered their names as we moved forward. Tama smiled and Roffe's eyes widened – neither had any idea what was in the jungle. Fear and curiosity mingled in their eyes.

Abruptly, Elias stopped. He was the oldest. No one questioned that he was the leader.

"We have to hide," he said softly. "They'll be coming soon to work the sugar cane fields. We can't let them find us."

"Are there monsters here like the crocodiles?" Tama asked.

"No. The monsters live on the shore."

Elias pushed a little further down the trail then turned off into jungle so dense it was nearly impossible to move. His arms were strong – he beat back huge leaves, tangled bushes, and snakelike vines so we could creep beneath. We didn't go very far; the jungle was so thick that once off the trail we were easily hidden.

Elias pointed to a cluster of rocks that burst through the jungle like a guardhouse in the forest. "We'll stay there for now until it's safe to move on. If we can't see the trail, then they can't see us."

"How will we know when we're safe?"

"I'll know."

I wondered how Elias learned those things but I remained silent. Who else was there to trust?

We scrambled on the rocks and huddled together beneath a sprawl of huge fern leaves. I tore off a few leaves, rolled them and made pillows for each of us. Tama and Roffe leaned against each other. Elias squeezed my hand.

"Sleep," Elias said, "I'll keep watch."

I settled Tama and Roffe on the leaves. They curled up and fell asleep immediately. I looked at Elias fighting sleep.

"Elias?"

"Yes."

"Do you think we're going to be okay?"

"We have to be."

"Why?"

"God's plan."

"Are you sure?"

"Of course I'm sure. I'm an Abravanel. I know these things."

Yet I saw doubt in his eyes. I leaned over and kissed him. Elias wrapped his arms around me in a fearless embrace. He kissed me and our bodies melted into one another. He searched inside my mouth with his tongue, arousing dizzying emotions.

"What's happening?" I pulled away, struggling to catch my breath.

"We're in love." His voice was thick. "I'm going to take care of you – and Tama and Roffe. And then . . ."

"What?"

"I'm going to make love to you."

"Make love?"

Elias grinned. "Marry you."

The idea of marriage while sitting on rocks in the middle of the jungle made me laugh. Elias looked doubtful then suddenly joined me.

"Everything is going to work out Esperanza. You'll see."

I touched the hamsa on my neck. Elias leaned over and moved my hand. Then he kissed the hamsa.

"We're protected," he said, his lips against the silver and his head on my chest.

I believed him with all my soul.

"Sleep. You need your rest. And while you're resting . . . look out for snakes."

"What? Snakes? Are they dangerous?"

"There are snakes in the jungle but if we're careful they'll leave us alone. They're not like people who *love* to hurt."

I knew he was talking about Simao. Elias would never say the name again.

I shook my head but said nothing.

"Sleep," Elias whispered, gently pushing me down on the rock. He held my hand.

3

My eyes snapped open. Everyone was sleeping. Elias, sitting stiffly on the edge of the rock, had drifted off, his breath slow and rhythmic. Good. He needed rest.

I was curled up on the rocks with the fern leaf unrolled. I didn't want to move and wake the others. Suddenly something moved. It was a green creature that looked like a fragile stem . . . long and thin, with transparent wings and delicate legs that edged noiselessly across the surface of a leaf. I think they called it a *mantis*. I watched as the creature made its way over the leaf and disappeared beyond the rocks. That was when I saw the flowers. They were the most beautiful purple flowers I had ever seen in my life. Some were tiny with flat petals and yellow-and-purple centers. Others draped down like purple cloth, held together with a green tip at the top. The prettiest were made up of uneven pale purple petals with dabs of pink in a delicate balance on a thin green stem.

Like us. Delicate but strong.

I'm going to make it. We're going to make it.

I was jolted by the new voice within me.

I heard a familiar sound. It was beyond the purple flowers, the cries of the birds, and the noisy clatter of the jungle. I stiffened. It rang *through* me. I looked at Elias. He was wide awake, his back stiff and his hand clenched into fists. He glanced at me and put a finger to his lips.

Stay quiet. No noise.

The sound began low and then grew . . . I recognized the unmistakable thud of human feet on a dirt trail. Voices, some harsh, some singing, filtered through the jungle. I thought I heard the Shema drifting in the canopy.

Shema Yisrael Adonai Elohaenu Adonai Echad

I realized it was Elias. Quietly, I said the words alongside him. He smiled.

I held my breath. I could hear them but not see them. The Shema couldn't make them go away.

"Silence," Elias whispered.

Tama and Roffe were suddenly awake.

"Silence," Elias said to them.

No one moved. If we were very quiet they would never know we were only steps away from them. Elias grabbed my hand and we waited. Tama hung onto one arm and Roffe crept very close. No one moved.

Time stood still.

Butterflies, in the most amazing colors, fluttered in front of my eyes. A tree frog, the color of limes, paused to stare at us with bulging orange eyes and then leaped away. A huge, hairy spider sauntered over the rock, his legs brushing against my ankle.

Watch, listen, and don't move.

"Did you hear that?" Someone called from the sugar cane work crew.

The feet paused.

"Hear what?" Another voice.

"That."

"I don't know what you're talking about."

"The missing kids. Maybe they're here?"

"Maybe they'll stay here," a voice whispered. "They killed a man."

"A pig. They killed a pig who raped the girls."

"It doesn't matter. He's dead and the girls are safe for now."

"Move on," the crew leader yelled over their heads.

"If you hear us," a voice whispered, "if you're here . . . may God go with you."

Elias and I stared at one another. He squeezed my hand. "May God go with you," he whispered into the jungle.

It took a long time before the human sounds faded and my breathing returned to normal. My shoulders sagged. I was suddenly aware of how rigid I became – how my whole body was frozen in place, feeling nothing but Elias's hand.

"We're fine for now," Elias said finally. "They didn't see us. We'll wait until they come back after their work for the day, heading for the compound. Then we'll own the trail."

"Why not follow another trail?"

"There's only one. It leads to the sugar cane field not far from here. On the other side of the field the trail continues but people don't go that far."

"Where does it go?"

"Deeper inland, away from the shore. That's what the degradados told me. It leads to the mountain's edge and then climbs . . ."

"To the fugitive camp?"

"I hope. I don't know anyone who ever took it that far and returned. We have to go deep into the jungle and up the mountain to find the camp."

"If it exists?"

"Yes, if it exists."

I struggled to gather my thoughts. "What if it's a story . . . that there really isn't a fugitive camp? What if we're all alone?"

Elias sighed.

"How will we know if we're going in the right direction?"

"We won't. If the fugitives are in the mountains, they'll find us long before we find them."

My hand trembled. Gently, Elias kissed my fingers. "We'll be okay. I promise."

I wondered how he could make a promise like that. But didn't I promise to keep Tama safe? Was taking her down an unknown jungle trail to an unknown fugitive camp mean keeping her safe? And if we found the camp, what if another Simao lived there?

4

We spent the day on the rocks, napping, telling stories, playing games with pebbles. Roffe and Tama cried that they wanted to leave – continue down the path that had now become an adventure rather than something to fear. Elias and I knew better. We were far from safe. At any minute faces could appear in the leaves. We would be surrounded, dragged back to the compound and . . . I didn't want to *think* about what they would do to us.

We waited quietly for the sugar cane crew to pass on their way back to the compound.

At one point in the day, Elias scrambled off the rock and disappeared into the jungle. He returned with a strange red-yellow fruit.

"What's that?" Tama asked.

"It's called a banana," Elias explained. He peeled off the thick skin and inside was a soft, pale yellow meat with a very sweet smell. "Try it."

Tama and Roffe refused. Tentatively, I took a small bite out of the soft flesh. It was the most delicious thing I had ever tasted . . . sweet, with an exotic flavor and a soft creamy texture. I finished it quickly and Elias laughed.

"Try it!" I encouraged Tama and Roffe.

Elias handed them each a banana.

Tama hesitated but Roffe bit into it, skin and all.

"Ugh," he cried and spit it out.

Elias laughed. "You're not supposed to eat the skin." We watched as he took Roffe's banana and peeled it from the bottom up. "Now try."

Reluctantly, Roffe took a small bite. His smile said it all.

We spent the rest of the day eating bananas, having banana skin fights, imitating the birds, and trying to catch butterflies. It was the first day we felt happy since they took us from our families in Portugal.

Hope shyly returned.

Late in the afternoon we heard the sugar cane crews returning from the fields. All of us froze. Tama and Roffe closed their eyes but Elias and I watched, listening to the voices and footsteps. We stayed that way for a long time after the noise faded and the jungle sounds took over.

"I think we're safe now," Elias said softly.

"For now," I shivered.

Tama and Roffe were afraid to speak.

The sun was low in the sky and the jungle darkening when we finally crawled from beneath the ferns and leaped off the rocks.

"They're gone. Let's get out of here."

Tama and Roffe didn't want to move. I took their hands and encouraged them to follow Elias. They trusted me as if I was their mama. We crawled through the jungle until we reached the trail. When they saw it was empty, Tama and Roffe sang and skipped across the dirt. Elias grabbed their arms.

"We still have to be quiet," he said sternly. "Until we know that we're completely safe."

Tama and Roffe stopped their games and nodded. No one wanted to return to the compound.

"Where do we go now?" I asked.

"Down the trail," Elias whispered. "We'll keep moving until we reach the sugar cane fields, cross them and continue on the other side. The sun sets late and there are streams on that side where we can get water, bananas, and other fruits. We'll rest and then keep on moving down the trail."

"Do you know where . . . ?"

Elias shook his head. "Don't ask that question. Just pray. *No one* knows where the trail goes."

I took his hand. "This is better than being in the compound and catching the fever and . . ."

Suddenly Elias turned. He pulled me into his arms and kissed me hard. I wrapped my arms around him and kissed back. I felt the old tension released – and a new, delicious pressure shared between lovers. Tama and Roffe watched, dumbfounded. I didn't want Elias to let me go – I wanted the moment to last forever. I clung to him with all my strength. Eventually he peeled my arms off his back and cradled my chin in his hands. We stared at each other and for an instant forgot where we were and what we had done.

Tama's voice broke the moment. "Are you married?"

We looked at her and laughed. She and Roffe joined us, a nervous confusion in their eyes.

"We're not married," Elias said. He took my hand, "but we will be."

"Yes." I kissed him on the cheek.

Tama clapped her hands. "Then you'll have Elias' baby not Simao's."

A picture of the man I murdered filled my mind, replacing the joy of Elias' embrace. I shuddered.

Never forget you're capable of murder.

"You did the right thing," Elias whispered, reading my thoughts. "He had to die or he would have continued to kill the Jewish girls."

I knew Elias was right.

Why me? Why was I the one who had to murder the snake to save the girls?

There were no answers. No turning back. It didn't matter who I killed – I was still a murderer. I had to live with the guilt. Elias watched with concern in his eyes.

"You have to make peace with it Esperanza."

I nodded. "Let's go."

Elias led us down the trail. We silently picked our way; hearts pounding even though we knew the work detail was already back at the compound. We reached the edge of the field just as the sun was setting. In front of us were rows of leafy plants with long, thin stalks that swayed gently in the breeze. We paused and stared at the empty field fenced by dense jungle.

"Taste this," Elias said and broke off a stalk for each of us.

I was hesitant but Roffe and Tama chewed on it eagerly. Their eyes lit up.

"*Caña de azúcar,*" Roffe cried. Sugar cane.

Hesitantly, I chewed on the stalk.

The sugar cane was sweet like candy – raw, juicy, and chewy. Grinning, I joined the others in our feast. Suddenly we heard an eerie squeal and thousands of creatures flew above our heads. They had angled wings and points, tiny black eyes, and spiky ears.

"Flying monsters!" Tama cried and tried to run away but Elias caught her arm in one hand and Roffe in another.

I was terrified. Were these people-eating monsters like the crocodiles?

Elias laughed. "It's a *bastao* – bat. They don't like us anymore than we like them. They won't hurt us."

He snared one to show us.

The bat was dirty brown, the color of rocks covered with loose soil. It had long, ugly wings and beady black eyes that stared straight through us.

I shivered. Tama and Roffe examined it without touching.

After several minutes, Elias threw it into the sky so it could join the others.

"Are there other monsters here?" Tama asked.

Elias shook his head. "The only big animals are ones that come in the carracks with people. Everything . . . except the crocodiles . . . are small and either crawl, jump, fly or creep along the jungle floor."

I didn't quite believe him.

"No one is left in the field now," Elias added. "Let's cross to the other side and pick up the trail. If we walk a little bit further I heard that there's a stream with fresh water and we can stay for the night. Tomorrow morning we continue along the trail before anyone gets to the field. They'll never find us."

"Who told you that?"

Elias didn't respond.

"Will they try to come after us?" Tama asked sweetly.

"No, we're safe now."

"Are you sure?"

Elias took a deep breath. "Who cares about a bunch of Jewish kids? No one would even bother to follow. They probably think we were eaten by the crocodiles."

But we're murderers.

I wanted to say the words, remind him that they might want revenge for killing one of their own. I said nothing.

Elias led us through the sugar cane field, buzzing insects, and bats. I was glad when we reached the other side. The trail led away from the field and further from the compound.

We followed the trail until we heard the sound of water. Elias broke through the jungle and led us to a stream with fresh, cold water. We were very thirsty and drank for a long time. When we finished, Elias pointed to a cluster of rocks on the other side of the stream.

"That's where we'll spend the night."

5

Once again, I was the first to wake up. In front of me was a small, hairy creature with a long, rat-like tail. I watched as it crawled over the rocks with four babies hanging on by their tails. It wasn't like the rats I saw on the Sao Gabriel – big, ugly gray rodents that lived in the hold and feasted on garbage. Sometimes, the sailors caught one and cooked it for dinner.

My stomach flip-flopped when I thought of the ship.

I looked up and watched the light trickle through the forest canopy. I was hungry. We had finished the bits of bread Tama gathered from the compound. We had nothing to eat but fruit, the "safe" greens that Elias recognized, and chunks of sugar cane. I wondered if we would ever taste bread or olives again, eat meat like Mama's Shabbat stew, or nibble on plump round chick peas.

"It's called a *megera* or shrew," Elias whispered over my shoulder, giving the rat-like creature a name.

"It looks like a rat."

He laughed softly. "I hope we never see a rat again."

"I hope we never see a monk again."

"I hope we never see a Portuguese again."

"I hope we never see Alvaro de Caminha again."

"I hope . . ." Elias grinned, "we never have to see any of them again."

We giggled.

Elias put his arms around me and we cuddled, savoring the closeness. I felt better – safer – when he held me.

Tama and Roffe stirred. We watched as they woke up into their strange new world. Elias kept his arms around me. They accepted us – even called us married. I think it made them feel safer as if their mamas and papas were still with them.

When Tama and Roffe were fully awake, we climbed off the rocks, leaving our leaf-beds behind us. First we drank from the stream. The water was cool and delicious. We were ready to move further away from the compound.

"Will we find the fugitive camp today?" Tama asked.

"I don't know," Elias replied. No one knew anything except that we had to go deeper into the island, climb higher up the mountain, and wait for them to find us.

We followed the trail for hours, silently trekking through the jungle.

Gradually, everything changed. We were engulfed in fog. The world dripped with water. The trees reached higher in the canopy – taller and thinner than the ones we saw earlier. It felt like we were walking in a dream, covered in delicate mist as if in a haze of our imaginations.

We paused and looked around. It was staggeringly beautiful.

"What is it?" I asked softly, afraid to speak too loud and break the vision.

"I've never been here," Elias whispered, "but one of the degradados told me about it. They call it the Cloud Forest. It means that we're much higher than sea level."

"Up the mountain?"

"Yes."

"In a cloud?"

"Kind of . . ."

Tama and Roffe looked up and tried to catch handfuls of mist. Their giggles were softened by the mist; their games looked like a fairy dance.

It was the strangest place I've ever experienced. Surreal and otherworldly. I wondered how God could create something like this . . . the same God who allowed evil men to kidnap children. The thoughts confused me so I pushed them from my mind, breathing in the Cloud Forest like it was a piece of legend.

Mama would have loved this.

Elias nudged us forward.

"We have to keep going."

Reluctantly, we focused on the trail, each step taking us higher up the mountain. The trail became steep and narrow, sometimes hard to follow. Not many human feet had passed before us. The fog and dreamy feel of the forest shifted our moods. Tama hummed a song. Roffe followed with a Spanish folksong about heroes. Our voices joined together muffled by the mist.

When King Nimrod
Went out into the fields
He looked into the heavens
And at all the stars
He saw a holy light.

A strange thing happened. Hope took over like a long lost friend. Elias held my hand as we climbed higher in the cloud forest and breathed the cool air. The trees were shorter and there was no longer a canopy that filtered the light above our heads. It felt good to breathe deeply and our footsteps were livelier. Tama and Roffe played tag – they were acting like children again.

The sun dipped in the sky and we reluctantly ended the day. We found a group of rocks near a cold stream surrounded by fruits. Tama, Roffe, and I prepared leaf beds as Elias collected fruit. He told us stories about brave men and beautiful princesses as we ate and the sun slowly set. We fell asleep blanketed by the mist.

6

I woke before the others. I was beginning to enjoy being alert while everyone slept. I expected to watch butterflies and shrews, listen to birds or the whooshing of leaves.

Instead, I saw two black human eyes emerging from the mist.

My heart pounded wildly. I threw out my arms and screamed as loud as I could.

Elias leaped up; Tama and Roffe cowered behind me.

The eyes retreated into the mist.

Did I dream them? I blinked my eyes, and peered through the fog.

Nothing.

"What's wrong?" Elias demanded.

"Did you see him?"

Elias searched the cloud forest with his eyes. "See who?"

"You?" I turn to Tama and Roffe.

They shook their heads.

"You must have been dreaming," Elias sighed. "If anyone was here, I would have seen him."

"You were sleeping."

"I would have heard. No one can be *that* quiet."

"They can if they want."

"We'll be more careful."

I backed down. "Let's get moving," I said lightly, hugging Tama. "I must have been dreaming."

The day passed like the one before – following the narrow trail, climbing through the mist, stopping to drink from sweet water streams that flowed downward toward the shore. We sang, ate fruit, and stopped to play. Again, Tama and Roffe played tag while Elias and I stole a few kisses. We held each other tighter, without abandon.

The old rules were dead.

There were no people – the only animals we saw were the birds, small creatures like shrews and geckos, and the constant buzz of insects. We found another outcropping of rocks and settled in for the night. When Tama and Roffe fell asleep, Elias crept close to me and cradled me in his arms. His hands wandered in the dark. He stroked my neck and then touched my breasts. I shivered. I should have pushed him away – yelled at him – but I didn't care. The only thing that was important was his body pressed against mine, his lips, and his fingers that sent jolts inside me. I felt his privates get hard. Like Simao?

"Is that what happens to men?"

Elias chuckled in the dark.

"Is it like the monthly blood for women?"

He hesitated. "There are men like him who use it to hurt women."

"Hanna?"

"Yes. But there are men – like me – who use it to show how much they love their woman."

"I don't understand."

"You don't have to – but when you're ready it will be a beautiful thing."

"When we marry?"

"Yes, my love. When we marry."

We fell silent, resting against each other. I stared into the dark and tried to keep my eyes open. I struggled to make sense of the thoughts racing through my head. What did Elias mean? Was I really his love? How could we ever marry in the middle of a jungle?

Fatigue won. I fell asleep.

I don't know how long I slept. Tama and Roffe were curled up on their leaf beds. Elias was sprawled on his back, holding my hand. I tried not to move but something startled me. It was very early and the sun was rising, piercing the leaves and trickling lazily in the mist. I dropped Elias' hand and sat up on the rock. That was when I saw the eyes again.

It was a slight, barely perceptible movement behind a cluster of large, sweeping leaves dripping with water. This time I knew that I wasn't dreaming.

The leaves moved again.

Maybe it's human?

Suddenly, a head poked out from between the leaves. They were the same black eyes I saw yesterday. It was a man with the darkest skin I had ever seen . . . darker than the black-olive colored men at the compound.

He seemed disembodied . . . only his head was visible. I wanted to scream again but something stopped me. It was his eyes. The black man was as scared as me.

We stared at one another for several minutes. I smiled but he didn't respond. Slowly he retreated back into the forest. Should I wake the others? I wasn't sure so I did nothing.

7

The days slipped into a routine. We walked, sang, ate fruit, and drank from the streams. The mist thinned and disappeared. We had no direction but the narrow path. No one was afraid anymore. I didn't tell them about the black man. They would probably assume I was dreaming.

Each night when Tama and Roffe slept, Elias and I explored our bodies above our clothes. I felt the powerful muscles on his shoulders and arms and stroked his long, lean legs. He touched my breasts. His hands were gentle and curious. One night he brought my hand to his privates. It was very hard. When I touched it he breathed heavily and clung to me tighter.

"My love," he gasped.

The days moved on. Elias and I waited for the nights.

Around us, the trees got shorter and more stunted. The air was cooler – steamy heat was left behind. It was clear that we were climbing higher each day. Every morning I saw the man's face. He crept closer as if less afraid. One morning he stepped from the brush and I saw that he was entirely naked except for a ragged loin cloth tied around his middle, covering his privates and a small pouch slung from his waist. His body was thin but muscular. I gasped. He saw that he had startled me and quickly stole back into the forest.

I knew that he was following us.

"There's someone watching," I said to Elias.

Elias nodded.

"You've seen him?"

"Very dark, slipping between the leaves?"

"Yes."

"He doesn't want us to see him."

"I saw him, Elias. He came out of the forest and stood in front of me."

"Did he try to hurt you?"

"No – he just looked. When he saw I was frightened he disappeared."

"I don't think he'll hurt you. Or any of us."

"Who is he?"

Elias shrugged. "I don't know. Maybe he's one of the African slaves. You know, taken from his home like we were."

"A fugitive?"

"Maybe."

"From the fugitive camp?"

"He could be a guard or lookout. Watching us as we get closer. He doesn't want to hurt us but they have to be sure we don't want to hurt them."

I never thought about *that*. The fugitives had to be as cautious and secretive as us.

"We're children. Why would he be afraid of us?"

"That's why he's just watching."

An icy chill ran down my spine. "Instead of . . ."

Elias stopped me before I said the words.

Instead of killing us.

"Should we do anything?"

"No, just wait and see what happens. Maybe he'll start to trust us."

In an instant, the forest was not quite as beautiful. It was fraught with danger, not from monsters but from *people*.

"Don't say anything to Tama and Roffe," Elias added. "Let's not frighten them."

We continued on the trail but Elias and I stopped singing with Tama and Roffe. We constantly looked around us. We didn't *see* the man but we sensed his presence. Mid-day we settled on a pile of rocks near a stream. Elias and I stood guard while Tama plunged into the mud puddles next to the water, laughing and splashing.

"A lura sosai!" The man screamed and leaped from the leaves, pulling Tama out of the mud. We rushed to protect her, our cries mingled with fear.

Tama wailed. She sounded like the children when the crocodiles tore them apart. I screamed. Elias raised his fists and Roffe's eyes were wild, not knowing what to do.

Tama's ankles were covered with fat worms.

The black man stopped us with his eyes. He set Tama on his knee and one-by-one, picked off the worms leaving behind trickles of blood. He tossed the worms back into the mud and pulled some leaves from the pouch on his waist. He wrapped the leaves around Tama's legs, balanced himself on the rocks, and cradled her like a baby, singing in a strange language.

No one moved.

Tama stopped crying as he sang. She nuzzled into his chest. The three of us stared, not knowing what to do.

"Leeches," Elias mumbled.

Slowly we approached the man. Tama was very quiet, her eyes closed.

The black man looked at us. "*Suna na . . .*" he said slowly. "*Nweke.*"

We stared at him. None of us had ever heard his language.

"Suna na . . ." he repeated. "Nweke." He pointed to his chest.

Tama opened her eyes. She wasn't afraid. She smiled up at him. He smiled back. His white teeth looked like a flash of light in his dark face. His eyes were gentle.

"Suna na . . ." he grinned. "Nweke."

Tama got it. "Tama," she said and sat up in his lap.

He smiled so hard that the white teeth took over his face. "Tama," he said slowly in a thick accent.

Tama slipped off his lap. "Nweke," she grinned.

Nweke peeked under the leaves he had wrapped around her legs. "Eh," he nodded and peeled them off, throwing each one into the brush.

There was no blood.

He bowed his head and turned to Elias. "Nweke," he pointed to his chest. His eyes changed. They weren't soft like when he spoke to Tama. They were firm and steady. Respectful.

"Elias," Elias pointed to himself.

Nweke struggled to say the name. He turned to me. I smiled. I felt like I had already met Nweke. "Esperanza," I pointed to myself. "It's good to meet you, Nweke.

"Ezz-pee" Nweke said.

"Yes!"

"Ezz-pee," he repeated.

Everyone cheered. "This is," I touched Roffe's shoulder, "Roffe."

Nweke nodded. He said the other names slowly, struggling with the sounds. Our names were funny with his accent. We laughed.

"Nweke . . . Ezz-pee." I clapped my hands.

"*Livre*," Nweke said in Portuguese.

Free.

"Livre," we agreed.

"Nweke . . . Ezz-pee livre." He grinned.

"Who is he?" I whispered to Elias.

"He's probably an ex-slave who ran away so he could be free."

"Livre," I said solemnly.

Nweke's face was serious. He said something in his language and I shook my head to show I didn't understand. Nweke took a deep breath and struggled with another Portuguese word.

"*Seguro*." Safe.

We didn't need any more words.

Nweke

1

We trusted Nweke. He was like flowers we found in the jungle. Strong. Beautiful. Exotic. Even though we spoke different languages, he understood. We were all refugees from the Portuguese. They would beat, enslave or kill us if we ever returned to the settlement.

Nweke led us off the trail. The air was cooler, the land more rugged, and the forest not as dense. We saw jagged peaks above the trees and knew that we were very high – far from the shore. I remembered my first view of São Tomé from the ship. The mountain seemed to emerge from the water, surrounded by dense jungle. We were now part of that mountain. The birds were still noisy and we often heard the *woo-woo* of owls that lived at this altitude. There were many cool streams but we knew to avoid muddy puddles where the leeches lived. Nweke showed us many things – fruits and greens we could eat; berries and roots we could dig up and cook over a fire. Nweke taught us how to make fire. Sometimes I tried to imagine what Nweke's life had been before the Portuguese made him a slave. I wondered if he lived in a tribe, if he was a chief or the son-of-a-chief. When he was wrenched from home and all he knew, did he leave behind a wife and children? What did it feel like to be chained, shipped to São Tomé, and forced to work for the Portuguese?

Nweke knew a lot about the mountain and the island. Elias and I still close together at night although we did not touch each other. We were afraid Nweke would disapprove. We learned from smiles and gestures that he didn't think we were bad.

Tama became very attached to Nweke. She liked to hold his hand when we moved through the forest and crawl in his lap when we rested. Nweke's eyes lit up and he treated her as if she was a daughter. Perhaps Nweke had a child like Tama in Africa?

We would never ask.

2

One night while Nweke, Tama, and Roffe were sleeping in our "camp" Elias woke me up.

He put his finger to his lips. "Ssssh. Follow me."

I scrambled to my feet. He took my hand and led me away.

"Where are we going?"

"It's time."

"Time for what?"

Elias didn't respond. We walked for several minutes until we reached a tiny clearing. He had scouted it out earlier. It was surrounded by trees and tiny flowers. The full moon bathed us in silvery light.

"Why are we here?"

Elias led me to a circle of tiny rocks. He paused and faced me, taking both my hands in his.

"There won't be any Rabbi for us," he said thickly. "No *Ketubah* – wedding contract. We'll never have a canopy or listen to songs and prayers from loved ones. You will never wear a veil or drink from a blessed cup of wine."

He eyes sparkled in the moonlight. "I can't give you anything but . . ." He held out a tiny ring woven from delicate vines. "Nweke showed me how," he grinned. "It won't last forever but it will work until I can find something better."

I stared at the ring. It was the most beautiful jewelry I had ever seen.

"Give me your hand."

I stretched out my left hand. Elias slipped the vine ring on my forefinger – the traditional wedding finger that was believed to reach straight to the heart.

"Behold my love," he chanted hoarsely, "you are wed to me by the rite of holy matrimony according to the Laws of Moses and Israel. Now, you say it to me."

A lump swelled in my throat. For a moment I couldn't recall the words. Elias prompted me – like so many brides and grooms had been prompted for thousands of years before us.

"Behold my love . . ." he whispered.

"Behold my love," I found my voice. "You are wed to me by the rite of holy matrimony according to the Laws of Moses and Israel."

He flung a tiny, hollowed coconut on the ground. Then he stomped on it until it shattered. He looked at me with a crooked grin. "My wife."

Mama. Papa. Hanna. Are you here? Do you see this?

I felt their presence and their blessing.

"My husband."

Gently, Elias pulled me to the ground within the circle of rocks. The moon smiled at us. He started kissing me, igniting a new fire in my body. He slipped off my clothes and I tried to hide my nakedness but he gently pushed my hands away.

"You're too beautiful to hide."

He kissed my face, my breasts, and my privates. My heart raced and I was dizzy with a different kind of heat.

"My beloved," he whispered over and over until it felt like a prayer.

He slipped out of his clothes and I saw his manhood. Simao and the soldiers bombarded our lovemaking. I was suddenly afraid. Elias *knew*.

"Simao and the others hurt. This is an expression of our love for one another – husband and wife – God's gift to us."

He guided my fingers to his manhood and let me explore it until I was no longer afraid. He kissed my nakedness until I felt only passion not fear. He kissed my hamsa. Then he slowly entered me. Two children became one.

We fell asleep naked in one another's arms.

3

I was afraid to return to camp. We dressed quickly. I wanted to relive the night, feel Elias' kisses and the passion when he entered me.

Elias smiled at my desire. "We have to go back."

"They won't understand."

"They will. I promise."

We headed back to the others. I knew that I was different – the light in my eyes had shifted and there was a new bounce in my step. I couldn't stop staring at the vine ring.

I paused on the edge of camp. "What do we say?"

"We don't have to say anything. They'll know."

"Know what?"

"That we love each other and we're now man-and-wife."

I doubted him until I heard Nweke's cry. He saw us and burst into a joyful melody in his own language. Tama and Roffe clapped their hands and cheered.

How did they know?

Tama and Roffe hugged us crying *"mazel tov."* Nweke tried the words but didn't come close. Sighing, he grinned and pounded Elias on his back. Their eyes met. They didn't need language to share their manly secrets.

We played, we sang, and we celebrated all day. We feasted on Nweke's strange food. Everyone wanted us to kiss, over and over again, clapping their hands at our touch. Tama stared at my vine-ring as if I were a princess wearing precious jewels. Roffe did dances that made us laugh.

It was a beautiful wedding celebration.

When day was settling and night moving in, Nweke nodded to Elias.

Elias led me back to the clearing and we made love, slowly, deliciously, and with more soul than any bride and groom ever possessed.

4

The next morning we resumed our journey.

I was intoxicated with Elias and our love-making. "Perhaps we *are* chosen," I whispered. He smiled and kissed my cheek.

After nearly a week as husband-and-wife, Nweke led the four of us to a clearing in the forest.

"Livre," he said in heavily accented Portuguese. "*Casa.*"

In front of us was a path of raised logs. Nweke stepped on one and waved his hand to follow.

Tama took his hand. Roffe followed.

Elias and I paused.

"Is this the forever part of our lives?"

"Yes, I think so."

"I'm scared. I don't know what to . . ."

Elias took me into his arms and kissed me. "We're doing this together. All of us. I promised it would be OK . . . and it will be. You won't ever have to worry about *him* again. It's over."

In my mind, I saw Hanna. I heard her cries and her silence. Then I saw Simao with his snakelike blue eyes, dirty caramel-colored hair, and rotted teeth. I heard his words.

I'm going to fuck you like you've never been fucked before. And when I finish, you know what you're going to say, my Jewish puta? Thank you. Thank you. Thank you.

"You killed him," Elias broke into my thoughts. "You killed the devil."

I took a deep breath and realized that Nweke, Tama, and Roffe were waiting for me.

"You're my wife now," Elias whispered. "Say the words."

Suddenly the horrors in my head shifted. They would remain there for the rest of my life in a corner of my memories. It was time to live today.

I clung to my hamsa, Elias, Tama, Roffe, and Neweke.

All of us, including Nweke, said the magical words.

Shema Yisrael Adonai Elohaenu Adonai Echad

Beyond
Broken
By
Kings

We stepped on the logs and followed Nweke. My hand, wrapped firmly in Elias', trembled. As we walked down the path, people emerged from the forest – dark black men, bare-breasted black women, mixed bloods with skin the color of roasted almonds, white men, ex-*degradados* with scars from the chains that bound them together, and white men with black women originally brought to the island as prostitutes. The people were silent as we passed them; they stared without smiles. At the end of the log path was a single, common hut with a thatched roof. We stopped.

The people gathered around us.

Nweke said something in his language and heads nodded.

A degradado, with only one arm and a wild, tangled beard stepped forward. "Who are you?" He demanded in Portuguese.

Elias spoke for all of us. "We're the Jewish children stolen from our families in Portugal, forced to come and colonize the island. This is my wife, Esperanza,and the children who traveled with us, Tama and Roffe."

The degradado turned to the others and translated. "How did you get here?"

"We ran away," I whispered. "The Portuguese . . . the monks . . . were very cruel."

Suddenly a woman with dark hair and dark eyes emerged. "I know," she lowered her head. "The Portuguese brought me here to be a whore."

We were silent. Tears filled my eyes.

"Red hair," the degradado grinned, "means good luck"

A cheer rose from the crowd.

"Is this the fugitive camp?" Tama asked.

"Yes."

"Can we live here?" Roffe said hesitantly.

The degradado laughed and translated for the others. Nweke grinned.

"It might not be easy, little one. And it's certainly not pretty but you're one of us now."

The degradado – and all the other people – opened their arms in welcome. My hamsa was warmed by them.

I was home.

The Broken Saga begins in 1492 when the Tapiador family is betrayed to The Inquisition. The daughters flee through a hidden trapdoor into a secret tunnel. The parents face the soldiers – decoys so their children can escape. Rozas and Lucas are dragged to the subterranean dungeons where people are tortured until they confess. What happens under the evil hand of the Inquisitors? Can Rozas and Lucas survive?

I see it clearly. Purple flowers shudder in the wind. Trees cry for rain. The sky fills with thin clouds that shape-shift as they pass overhead. A bird cloud suddenly transforms into a handsome *trovador*; a child cloud drifts into a crouching man. Suddenly there's a dull thud; a large cow with dark, soulful eyes faces me. I've seen this creature before; she's visited my dreams many times. I reach out to touch her and the sky turns black; the clouds scatter in terror.

I scream, but no sound is heard.

It's a dream that peppers my life, triggered by bits I sense, but can't always identify. It's strange and comforting, both at the same time.

Now I know the source.

The meat.

Read all the books in the Broken Series

Haunted family trees, chilling photo insights, and twisted psychopaths burst into life, blending fact, fiction, and photos into riveting stories you'll never forget.

Go to www.hauntedframilytrees.com/books or amazon.com to purchase these bestsellers in ebook, print (black & white), or collector's edition (full color print).

Amazon #1 Bestsellers!

Evil rises. Mack aimed the white gun at the stage. The shot blasted through the studio, reverberating off lights, cameras, and booms. For an endless moment no one moved. A red hole appeared on her forehead. Her eyes widened in confusion as blood spattered her cream-colored Armani suit . . .

Evil is born. Joshua enters the world in a gritty basement apartment beneath the shadow of an old water tower. He was beaten, neglected, and by the end of his first day of life, abandoned. Joshua's bone-chilling story is followed from the womb through foster care, and into the terror of his forever home.

Evil Grows. Everyone is terrified of Joshua. Drowned cats, dissected squirrels, and burning dogs are his playthings. No one knows what the child thinks or will do next. The Senator, Aldi and Cal, Sage, and Grandma Espie, return in this blood-curdling thriller.

Go back in time to discover where evil thrived in the past. Meet the ancestors of the characters in the first three Broken Books and follow their haunted family trees.

Evil Lurks. Enter the 17th century when Dutch New Amsterdam is run by tight-fisted Peter Stuyvesant. Twenty-three Jews arrive from Recife, Brazil, fleeing the Portuguese Inquisition. They face an agonizing struggle for their rights. Suddenly a psychopath surfaces, threatening everyone in the young settlement. The Dutch blame the atrocities on a gentle Munsee Indian while mutilated animals and children stain Jew's Alley. Who is the psychopath? Why is he or she attacking Jews? *Broken By Madness* blends fact, fiction, and photos into a riveting story you'll never forget.

Evil Spreads. Hannah and Esperanza flee The Inquisition, joining the expelled Spanish Jews in 1492. They find refuge on a tiny Portuguese farm with two old Christian peasants. A traveler discovers the sisters and turns them into the royal soldiers. Simao, a psychopathic soldier and his band arrive on the farm and evil spreads. How can the young girls survive the men?

Evil Evolves. Esperanza is kidnapped by the King's soldiers. She joins a group of 2000 Jewish children shipped to the malaria-infested African island of Sao Tome. The Portuguese soldiers in the camp are brutal, taking children as their sex slaves. Esperanza and her friends endure only to be grabbed by the newly arrived psychopathic soldier, Simao. Can they escape the fever and evil of kings?

Evil at home. The Broken Saga begins in 1492. The Tapiadors are Conversos (Secret Jews) who are betrayed to The Inquisition. Armed soldiers arrive to arrest them. The parents push their two daughters through a hidden trapdoor to a tunnel that leads to safety. The soldiers drag the parents to the torture chambers. Can the parents save their children and survive the torture?

Is there a psychopath in your life? Go to

http://hauntedfamilytrees.com/
haunted-family-trees-landing/

to sign up for your FREE copy of Dr. Fink's ground-breaking guide.

Discover the secrets of haunted family trees – from the infamous to your own . . . Go to

http://hauntedfamilytrees.com/
haunted-family-trees-landing/

to get stories that will amaze you, the truth in facts and photos, and the latest info about family curses and bizarre behavior.

Do you love photo insights? Go to:

http://hauntedfamilytrees.com/
landing-page

to get a free image each week in your email that will enlighten, inspire, and make you feel good.

Meet the Book People

Dr. Jeri Fink, author and photographer

I was eight years old.

Faces were penny candy – endless shapes and flavors. Colors throbbed in rhythmic neon lights. My world was a rush of stories written in black-and-white composition books.

There were so many ways to *see* things. The Oak outside my window was big and powerful – or shaky, like a typical New York City tree. I could take a sliver of black charcoal and make the same tree magically come alive on paper. My characters moved through plots more animated than the people next door. I aimed my camera and shot images that no one else noticed. They called me a free spirit.

I trained as a Family Therapist/Social Worker to help people negotiate their lives. I worked with everyone from "normal" to psychopath; individuals and couples to families. I also traveled the world, learning about different cultures and environments, seeing how much we're all alike – and how much we're different. And I published 28 books.

The Internet became my prized tool where I was able to merge the concept of psychology into psychotechnology. The same integration occurred in my photography – I call it photo insights. It came together in my writing – *The Broken Series* – where I merge fiction, photo insights, and psychology into fast-paced reads.

The series includes seven books – thrillers that explore haunted family trees, psychopaths, and their prey. The first three take place in modern times; the last four are historicals.

My blogs, photo insights, and email lists can be found throughout the internet – where the impossible becomes possible and the journey never ends.

Welcome to my world.

Please visit me at my website www.hauntedfamilytrees.com or email me at jeri@hauntedfamilytrees.com

Derek Murphy, book and cover designer

Derek Murphy started a book editing company while working on his PhD in Literature, but soon began using his background in fine arts to help clients with their book covers. Derek believes in using art to create an immediate emotional connection with readers, and get them invested in your story before they even open the book. Check out Derek's website at:

www.creativindiecovers.com

Thanks!

How do you thank everyone who was part of a project that spanned six years, eight books, and tens of thousands of photographs? It's a daunting job. If I leave anyone out please forgive me – there is an overwhelming number of people who have been part of my life and work during the creation of the *Broken Books* series.

First, my husband
Ricky Fink, always smiling even when I drifted into different centuries in the middle of dinner.

My children and their children:
Russell, Laura, Mason, and Emma Fink
Stacey, Johnny, and Nicky Rossi
Meryl and Tony Waters

My extended family:
Harvey Fink
Herbert Michelson
Barbara & Chris Woolley

Many thanks to my friends and supporters who listened to my stories, drowned my troubles in chocolate and sushi, and were always there when I needed them. Jay Braiman, Dr. Barton Cohen, Joyce & Joel Feldman, Dr. Edward Fryman, Pat & Mary Ann Hannon, Howie Hutchinson, Janet & Rich Kam, Bill Komar, Jerry & Jill Lash, Dr. Carol Levy, Joan Mirabella, Barbara Saks, and John Viollis.

Special appreciation goes to my readers: Fern Friedman, Laura & Russell Fink, Craig Oldfather, and Dr. Sandra Roth; my experts: Nancy Allegretti, Mary Ann Hannon, and Margaret Mendel; my designer, Derek Murphy; my web developer Sonny Day; my social media director, Rachel Teplin; and my copy editor, Pat Hannon.

Thanks to Sue and Ken Yaeger, who generously shared their experiences and insights to bring these books alive.

Last, but far from least my co-author in the first three *Broken Books*, Donna Paltrowitz, who remains my friend and muse.

My gratitude goes to the many artists, authors, filmmakers, investigative reporters, photographers, psychologists, researchers, social workers, theorists, videographers, and online buddies who informed my work, empowering me to accomplish my mission.

In loving memory of Judy Becker, Persis Michelson, Dora Eisenstein, Edna Fink, Ruth Roth, Sandra Roth, and Vincent Meo.

Thanks to my readers who joined me in this amazing journey, on and offline.